The Canyon of Gold,

Buffalo Bill Cody,

and the

Legendary Iron Door Mine Treasure

By William T. "Flint" Carter

Volume I

Tucson, Arizona

"The Canyon of Gold Buffalo Bill Cody and the Legendary Iron Door Mine Treasure," By William T. "Flint" Carter

Cover: A real Iron Door Mine is finally discovered.

Produced and published with assistance from Robert Zucker, BZB Publishing, Inc. Tucson, Arizona. Phone: 520-623-3733. Email: publisher@emol.org

Photographs property of William T. Carter. Buffalo Bill Cody images, and letter, courtesy of the Buffalo Bill Museum and Grave in Golden, Colorado

http://www.buffalobill.org

ISBN: 978-1-939050-12-0

Contact Flint Carter:

Phone: 520-289-4566

Email: flintcartergold@gmail.com

Web: http://emol.org/flintcarter

This volume is dedicated to

William Frederick Cody

In honor of his 171st birthday.

Special thanks to Jill, Janis, and Robert Zucker,

whose work made this happen.

The Canyon of Gold
Buffalo Bill Cody
And The
Legendary Iron Door Mine Treasure

Table of Contents

First, let me say a hardy thanks to all those who have been part of my life in this CANYON OF GOLD adventure!

My name is William Thomas Carter II, aka – "Will" – "Bill" – "Tom" – "The General" – "Flint" (an alias for a spark of genius) – "The Count of Catalina," (sometimes "That No Account," but we know what counts is not always money) –  "Too Loose Cartier" – "The Confederate General of Big Sur" – "Wind Song Star Feather Thunder Roll" – "Ognon, The Show-be" (the richest man in the world) – and a few cuss words that we will leave out.

Please remember that I am not a professional writer— just an old prospector with a story to tell. But, I think someone might enjoy my tale, in my own words, no matter how it is presented.

From the beginning, the crux of the epic legend is Gold.

There is a saying that gold does not breed co-operation, and therefore, any research will yield outrageous and highly controversial assumptions.

Joseph Michael has a line in a song called "Gold Town" which says "Gold still glitters in the ground, hidden secret, like a laughing clown."

As most can imagine, anything gold on the surface is gone, along with the huge galleries mined by large corporations underground.

For millenniums, mankind has ground and smelted any rock even thought to contain gold. Most deposits are now depleted.

Today the heavy yellow metal is valued around $1,000.00 an ounce compared to $8.00 when the Anglos started coming to this area– the Santa Catalina Mountains.

"The Prospector," art by Flint Carter

Stories of the Canyon of Gold

Access to the Canyon of Gold.

I f you found a rich gold deposit what would do? You would not leave the gold uncovered for someone else to find.

This has not made it easy to find– especially when people purposely have hidden their treasures!

The trained eye can sometimes see things most would miss, but, with the progress in technology and easily obtained mineral maps– the rest is leg work.

However, the majority of hidden mines will never be found.

In the 1930s, the Civilian Conservation Corps (better known as the CCC) went into the Santa Catalina Mountains and cleaned up the Canyon of Gold. Since there had been no prior trash pick-up or sanitation, it was a toxic cesspool. Many mine tunnels were covered over.

Some say this took place all over the U.S. for the covert purpose to control the large mineral deposits from foreign interests and world control of the metals market.

THE MONKEY WRENCH GANG, by Edward Abbey, is a good example of certain resistances in the area. Ed wrote many books, including DESERT SOLITAIRE, and was considered by some to be the modern-day Henry David Thoreau.

The history one has been told– and has not been told– is so far from the truth that it hurts when one thinks about future generations.

Whatever has been said is misinformation– the largest stumbling block I have encountered in this project.

That is why this is called HISTORIC FICTION. Many of these learned facts are not true or provable but all in all it has been a fun life and history making!

Exploring the Canyon of Gold

This is when the fun began!!!!! Here I was– at the entrance to the legendary Canyon of Gold.

This should be easy, right??

Little did I know I was about to be a liar standing next to a hole in the ground.

But little did I care. I had found the gold and silver.

First, a little background.

Flint Carter standing at that hole in the ground.

The Rainbow Ranch

At the beginning of the 1970's, I bought one acre of land with a 12-foot by 20-foot chicken coop along the Cañada del Oro– the Canyon of Gold– at the edge of the Santa Catalina Mountains near Tucson. It sat between two old adobes on a man-made lake called Golder Dam.

The property was at the corner of the Canyon of Gold where the entire deserted canyon drains and the stream used to run nine months of the year.

The epic grandeur of the uninhabited legendary Canyon of Gold created the feeling of stepping back in time to when the original pioneers first came looking for gold and silver.

I called this spot Rainbow Ranch– after seeing a double rainbow upon arrival.

A six-mile long drive to the Ranch fostered a sense of safety; one could hear a car coming from miles away. But

The image of St. George slaying the dragon.

getting supplies to this desolate place was very expensive.

For one of the windows in the building, I salvaged from an old church a stained-glass pane of St. George slaying the dragon, a symbol of man overcoming unknown forces.

Over four decades later, I was the only one who had bought, stayed, and built on that land.

The nearby lake was 365 acres and 120 feet deep. A dam was built on a fault called the Pirate Fault, and when it was full, it started piping. From the pressure, it built 60-foot ant hills like sand piles along with water all the way to Oro Valley.

Because it was built backwards by the Army Corp of Engineers, it is now gone. Eventually, the dam was removed to allow for the massive retirement housing development called Saddlebrooke.

While the dam was being constructed, Hollywood filmed a movie there called "What If They Gave A War And No One Came" with Tony Curtis and Brian Keith. Another B-grade biker movie was done at the site later in the 1960s.

Originally Lloyd Golder's parents had purchased the 50,000 acres in 1959 for a dollar an acre. Lloyd and I had a written contract allowing us to search his land for the elusive Mine with the Iron Door and to recover any evidence.

Lloyd's father had a home just west of Campbell Avenue

and he sold his guest house to actor Lee Marvin. Lee was a star until he did a movie about a drunk, killing elephants for ivory. That was the end of his career.

Sadly, he died shortly thereafter. But, he will always remain a star, especially because of the movie "Paint Your Wagon" with Clint Eastwood, the only musical production made about prospecting.

When first built, the Saddlebrooke Home Owner's Association (HOA) did not allow any solar or alternative energy concepts or anyone under the age of 55. I was told by the previous land owners that the HOA wanted to stop me from making any claims on the land. It seems that the new residents were now the experts on the history of the area, and those who worked for decades to preserve the history– and lived it– were left out and forgotten.

The Solar Chicken Coop

After studying Design at Southern Illinois University under Buckminster Fuller, I was on a mission.

I planned to build a self-sufficient home that would heat and cool itself and provide a supplemental food source by farming the structures' walls inside and outside.

The plan was to have kinetic, thermal, wind, and solar energies and provide 200 miles a day of pollution free transportation.

After purchasing the chicken coop property, we implemented a natural stone earth sheltering and black sand iron into the building structure.

When I arrived in Arizona with an Inca gold Viking ski boat, I thought the hot desert never got cold. Much to my surprise, the chicken coop was the only shelter from the bitter desert cold.

A younger Flint Carter in the 1970s holding a rifle at the Rainbow Ranch in front of the chicken coop in the Cañada del Oro foothills of the Santa Catalina Mountains.

The solar coop is documented by the Arizona Governor's office as Arizona's first solar heated and cooled museum.

No one, at that time, had built anything similar into a building structure.

During the energy crunch, I was fortunate enough to get encouragement during a meeting with University of Arizona professors who agreed that my plan would work.

Building correctly would allow American citizens to be truly INDEPENDENT and FREE, as our founding doctrines proclaim, unlike the dependence endeared by the current inefficient and corrupt system powered by greed.

Our children's future depends on systems that nature can very well provide for free.

August 3, 1987

To Whom It May Concern:

This letter is written as a recommendation for
Mr. William T. Carter, whose address is CRB 8835,
Tucson, AZ 85738.

Mr. Carter has been involved in the history of the
Canyon del Oro valley and the foothills of the West
Catalina mountains, located near Oracle, Oracle Jct.,
and Catalina, for the past several years.

He is very conversant with the "Iron Door Mine" and
the Iron Door Legend Society. He has spent most of
his adult life promoting this legend, and this area.

Mr. Carter, at present, owns the mineral rights to
many hundreds of acres in this area, and is cogni-
zant of the rich heritage and potential use of the
many types of ore located on his claims.

He also developed the first solar heated museum for
Arizona. This is located in what was once a prominent stage stop servicing Oracle and Tucson. Many
miners lived in the area, as well as Catholic Priests
who built a small chapel similar to San Xavier del Bac.
The building is still standing.

But perhaps Mr. Carter's greatest achievement is the
idea of solar power to reduce tragedies on ice-covered
bridges. He enjoys a tremendous intellect for solar
power, and wants to be able to employ these ideas to
benefit mankind.

I consider Mr. Carter a very special friend, and am
determined to help him as best I can.

P 11

Sam Udall
607 South Gilbert Road
Gilbert, Arizona 85234

Letter from Sam Udall, Gov. Meacham's education aide
regarding the solar chicken coop.

21

The professors said it would take $350,000,000 to set up the casts and dies for the whole solar project to implement at the time. But, the math is simple. If present building continues there will be no farming areas left!!

All across the nation housing developments are consuming the farm lands as fields are being depleted for housing. More mouths to feed with less area to feed them. Something has to be done before it is to late!

This was 45 years ago and my message still is being ignored. The powers that be want us connected to the grid so they can profit and control us.

I became the first to mine using solar energy in the Catalina Mountains. There were two 12-volt car batteries, an electric fuel pump, and a two-foot square solar panel. I mined approximately 37 tons of water a day at an average of seven parts per million.

Saddlebrooke's History That You Don't Know

The area where the Cañada del Oro River feeds out at the west side of the Santa Catalina Mountains has been studied, explored, and documented. It is rich with history and legend; this is the famed Canyon of Gold.

The Motorola Executive Institute gave part of that area to the University of Arizona for the Biosphere. I initiated an archeological survey to document nearby carvings that overlooked miles of pre-historic irrigation canals for farming. They were dated to be between 4,000 and 6,000 years old. Sadly, they are now gone, but a photo I saved preserves its history.

This area was also the estate of Mariano Samaniego, a pioneer and one of the University of Arizona's first Regents, who had a mine, a store, and a freight line at the Ranch.

One of the petrogylphs that once stood at the edge of the
Canyon of Gold. All of them have been removed.

Mariano Samaniego

In 1911, below the Biosphere, George Stone Wilson started the Linda Vista Guest Ranch, formerly called Rancho Linda Vista. It was Arizona's first guest ranch consisting of two old adobe houses.

One building is believed to be Mission Santa Catalina of Jesuit origin. I spent many years restoring and studying this historic building.

The property was acquired through back taxes from the Mariano Samaniego family for whom the western ridge is named– Samaniego Ridge.

Marino Samaniego, born in 1844 in Sonora, Mexico, was a prominent Tucson pioneer. He arrived in Tucson in the mid-1860s and became a freighter, cattle rancher, merchant, and a successful Hispanic public official during the territorial period in the 1890s. The Samaniego's started the Hispanic Rights Movement.

The mission at the ranch before it was restored by Flint.

The mission building after restoration in the mid-2000s.

Samaniego was one of the founders and president of the Alianza Hispano-Americana, and was President, Vice President, and Director for the Arizona Historical Society. He served four terms in the Territorial Assembly, on the County Board of Supervisors, on the Tucson City Council, and as Pima County Assessor.

Burton Holly

The old man who sold me the property in the 1970s, Burton Holly, told me I was sitting on the biggest gold mine in the West.

Being in my '20s, I kind of thought the old man was just spinning yarns, especially when he told me he had built Hollywood, California, and had put up the sign that said "Hollywood Land." He told me that one day a rain storm had washed the word "Land" away. When people started moving in, they just called the area "Hollywood."

Little did I know how great of this man he really was. Holly had built 27 air bases in Canada and cut the timber for the Burma railway. He and Howard Hughes had ground the rivets off their plane and had also crossed the the Atlantic Ocean two weeks after Lindy in 12 hours less time. This accomplishment got them all the government contracts for the mail. That was where the money was at the time.

When Holly owned the ranch, it had an orchard of rare delights. There was a tree planted by Luther Burbank for Rita Hayworth's martinis. This tree, along with an orange tree, is all that survives today.

Holly had purchased the property from Lloyd Golder who told me that the inner Cañada del Oro area had saloons and hotels and was largely populated at the beginning of the 20th century.

Holly told me that after the *"Mine with the Iron Door"* film was made and during the Depression more than 10,000 people were making a meager living from the great Cañada del Oro– Canyon of Gold. Strangely, Holly died the day after I sold the ranch (one of many supernatural happenings of which I was an unknowing part).

The Linda Vista Guest Ranch

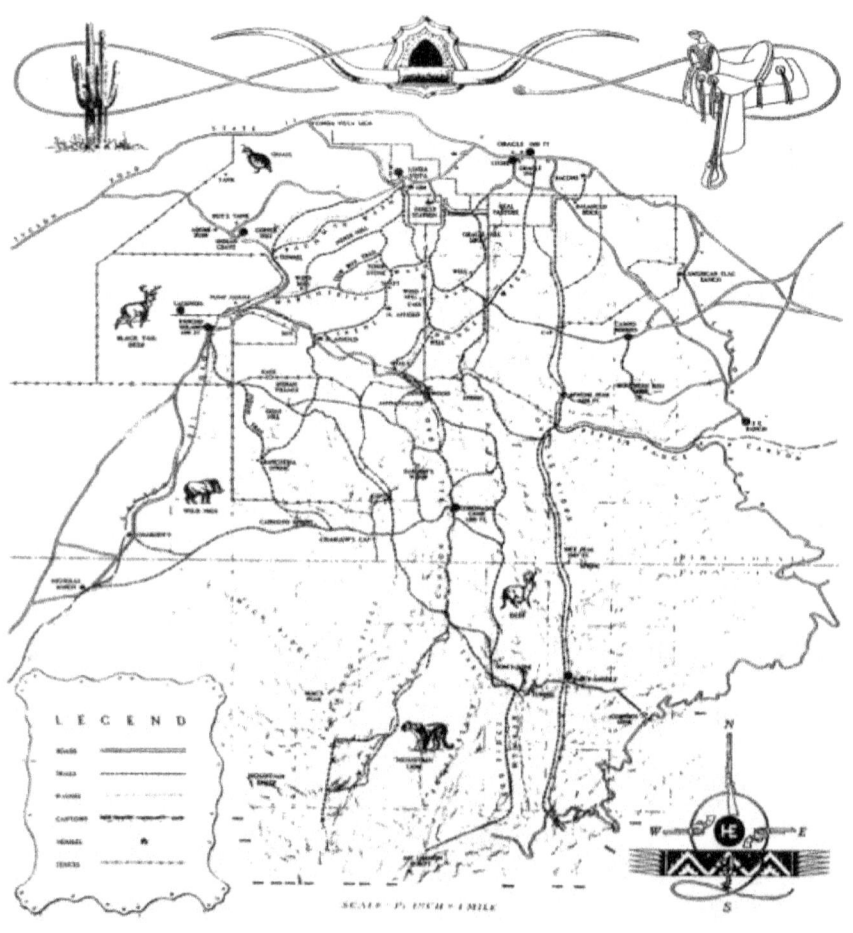

Map of the Linda Vista Ranch, Arizona's first guest ranch.

Arizona's first guest ranch and Mission Santa Catalina.

T he first guest ranch in the State of Arizona was the Linda Vista. It was the site of the first motion picture in Sonora, *"The Mine with the Iron Door,"* filmed by Sol Lesser of Principal Pictures, later Columbia Pictures.

The Linda Vista was also an ancient mining site with miles of irrigation canals dating back 10,000 to 11,000 years.

This time line is based on the Snake Town site, roughly 30 miles from the ranch. Dug by University of Arizona Prof. Emil Haury, it is where the Cañada del Oro meets the Santa Cruz River.

Art by Flint Carter.

The property was also a Cavalry picket post in the mid-1800s and was used for malaria victims from Fort Grant located just north at

Dudleyville.

In fact, the first pow wow between the Apache and Anglo settlers was held in this location in the 1860s.

In this historic event, over 1,000 Apache Indians, including 600 women and children, showed up in the Canyon of Gold from Arivipa.

Before Golder acquired the property at the Cañada del Oro, it was sold in 1911 by Harry Drachman, a Tucson tax collector, for $6.59.

The University of Arizona Farms, at River and Campbell, later sold for $12.33 in back taxes.

It is now owned by developers and is being developed for real estate– meaning, history will be lost forever.

The Casa del Oro

The 8th Wonder of the World, the Biosphere, was owned by the Motorola's Executive Institute in late 1970s. It was not far from my Rainbow Ranch and had the only phone in miles. Dr. Baker, who ran the Institute, allowed me use of the office and consulted with me on my project over the years.

Before the Institute was built, this property was the Casa Del Oro (House of Gold). It belonged to the Countess of Suffolk, a concert pianist. An old timer in the area, local prospector Buster Bailey, told me he had hired the once-famous Ira Hays, one of the Iwo Jima flag raisers, to dig the well for the Countess. Ira died shortly thereafter. As the old song says, "call him drunken Ira Hays, he won't answer anymore– not the whiskey drinking Indian, or the marine who went to war." Before the countess, Tucson dentist Doc Lackner was the first one to live on the ridge above the Ranch. The doctor used the gold and silver mined from the Catalinas in his dental practice.

Peppersauce Canyon

A good book on the area is ARIZONA HOOF TRAILS, by Elisabeth Lambert Woods who donated the Peppersauce Camp to the Salvation Army.

According to her final wishes, the property was not to be mortgaged or sold, and it was to be used for underprivileged children.

However, the property was eventually mortgaged and sold. The interesting part is that the covenant also stipulated that the spring at the site was never to be disturbed.

Could the spring be the entrance to unknown caverns?

Wherever there is moving water, there is inevitably erosion that over the eons causes voids. For example, when drilling for the Oracle Ridge Mine haul road, 200 foot caverns were encountered. To compare, Kartchner Caverns largest room is 120 feet high.

The San Pedro Valley

An article in the *"Arizona Daily Star"* newspaper in the 1930s states that items identical to those found in King Tut's tomb were found in the San Pedro Valley.

Five Indian villages on the bluffs above the San Pedro River from Alder Canyon north to Mammoth are now gone due to mining activities.

Only one site was studied by the University of Arizona, but, the report was never published. The villages were fair sized and had round buildings like Tusigood in Northern Arizona. One can still see 1,000-year-old dry farming fields on certain parts of the bluffs.

In the past, the first roads were the dry river beds used by boats or wagons. Buffalo Bill Cody, who had a mine in the Santa Catalinas, had his claims roughly 10 miles from a major transportation route. This was along the mineral formation called the Kalamazoo– the largest ore body in North America.

This is a photo of a huge stone monolith at the entrance to the Oracle Ridge Mine is thought to be Ionian script and about 2,800 years old. There was a similar monolith ten miles east along the San Pedro River. It was larger– 10 feet tall. But, it was bulldozed over while building the road. Flint is pictured second from the right with his hand resting on the monolith.

Oracle– the mining town

Oracle, Arizona, is located north of Tucson in the Southwest USA, on the northern slope of the Santa Catalina Mountains. The town was the named after the ship that pioneer and prospector Albert Weldon sailed to America when he began mining in the area on the northern foothills of the Santa Catalinas.

An earlier name for Oracle was Summit Springs from a battle that Buffalo Bill Cody and his scout William Neil fought together in Colorado. Both men lived in Oracle for a time.

There was a young outlaw activist ecologist, who ended up a professor of literature and wrote many books about the desert and its sensitive environment. It is said Ed Abbey only had a post office box in Oracle and did not actually live there although he actually died in Oracle. In the early days, he was an outlaw and kept a low profile. Abbey visited the Canyon of Gold in the Catalina Mountains many times and signed in on my Cabin Roster several times.

Little known but largely involved, Oracle has been the epicenter for over a century of a literary and film adventure– still alive and growing– concerning gold.

Many heard of the Mine with the Iron Door legend and some know about the film by the same name. It was shot in and around Oracle, Arizona, and was based on the book by Harold Bell Wright.

Freight lines near Oracle late 1800s.

Harold Bell Wright

At Coronado Camp where Harold Bell Wright wrote THE MINE WITH THE IRON DOOR. Pictured are Ron (left) and Nan Ingram, and Flint (in the shadows) in 1973.

Harold Bell Wright an author of the early 20ᵗʰ century, stayed deep in the inner Canyon at Coronado Camp, just over the Samaniego Ridge to the east of Saddlebrooke,

In 1917, the year that Buffalo Bill Cody died, George Wilson let Harold Bell Wright stay at the Coronado Camp where he wrote the book THE MINE WITH THE IRON DOOR.

The novel was made into one of Arizona's first Western movies of the same name. Wright brought the movie industry to the local Linda Vista Ranch in 1923 to film the movie, *"The Mine with the Iron Door."* He used local stories from his book which later was filmed at the site.

He was the first author in the United States to sell over a million copies of a book other than the Bible.

The first motion picture John Wayne starred in was *"Shepard of the Hills,"* another Harold Bell Wright book turned in to a motion picture.

The area surrounding Wright's other home on Tucson's eastside has streets named with the titles of his books.

Harold's son, Norman, continued in the true wild western fashion of his father. He helped Walt Disney produce Bambi, Fantasia, and the Wonderful World of Disney.

It is said when Harold Bell Wright was a preacher in Branson, Missouri, he was told to lock the church door he always had left unlocked. Wright replied, "Where I come from, God's door is never locked."

There is a Harold Bell Wright Museum in Branson that has more artifacts on display from this area than exist here.

Harold Bell Wright became Tucson's largest charitable benefactor.

Especially for Tucson, Wright created plays for local charitable events and brought in top actors. Proceeds went to charities.

He brought in stars from Hollywood to Tucson, like William Hart and Emma Carras of the Zigfield Follies. His play, "The Salt of the Earth," was a huge event back then.

Wright also started the local indigent health care program.

At the Tucson Medical Center, he began a tent city for tuberculosis victims. Wright also donated the furniture for St. Mary's Hospital.

The Tucson Kiwanis Club, a charity supported by Wright, was to erect a 30-foot marker at the entrance of the mine, but no records remain of where, or if, it was placed.

The Iron Door Mine

The Mine with the Iron Door has been one of the most extensively hunted lost mines in North America. Several movies and books have glorified this legend.

In less than a few hours from a bustling million inhabitants of the modern city of Tucson, Arizona, lies slumbering the centuries old legend the Iron Door Mine and its fabulous treasure. Centuries of production in gold and silver bullion still lie concealed in a mine of equal value.

Its real riches have yet to be revealed. That legend, though, may have some truth buried with those treasures. Some people over the centuries claimed to discover its location.

The exact spot of this treasure has never been documented.

To date, estimated mineral reserves in the general area in the Santa Catalina Mountains alone would pay the national debt twice over.

Little do most people know that the atrocities that have occurred in search of the elusive yellow metal.

Our Canyon of Gold is a good example of the things people will do for gold.

In the novel, MINE WITH THE IRON DOOR, you will remember Sonora Jack's style of the "old fire on the chest" to find the location of the gold. Spaniards were rumored to burn out the slaves eyes with red hot pokers to stop escape, because eyesight was not required in the lightless tunnels.

"Odie Faulk's Arizona," a short history, states Indians killed over 100 people and retired toward the Santa Catalinas, north of Tucson.

To date, it seems there was at least five iron doors.

In one story, they were called the Queens Doors. Legends are connected to an Iron Door in Kansas, Jesse James and the Knights of the Golden Circle.

There is a military reservation site in Kansas– with no access allowed– just as with the Victorio Peak military reservation, and bombing range in New Mexico that hold great treasures.

This legendary worlds' largest land treasure tied to the Canyon of Gold is a vast literary and film adventure for all to share.

People had heard of this fabulous treasure in Europe in the 1880s and had come to America to find THE LEGENDARY IRON DOOR MINE.

IRON DOOR MINE

The Story of Gold

BY WILLIAM T. CARTER

In the Canyon of Gold my story is a small one compared to this majestic mountain range and the past participants of its history. In the beginning, I knew nothing of gold or the desert and its mountains. It is now going on 14 years since I first came to the Canyon of Gold and I have learned that the truth is stranger than fiction.

I have been told by many people to put my story in print and have very leery to do so, simply because it is too unbelievable, and every day I learn more. By the time you read this, some of it will probably be outdated by new research and conjecture.

I will, however, to the best of my ability share with you my adventure and the truths as I see them.

The Gold I came searching for was peace and isolation, not profit. The world nor I, at the time, was interested in gold as it is today. The price was then $30 an ounce and had been since the government put a freeze on the price in the 1930s.

Subsequently, most of the actual mining was 40 years before I arrived, and much of human endeavors had been reclaimed by nature and time. Only a well-educated eye today can trace the ancient workings and no one will see it all.

Over the years, I've encountered many geologists with my story and shiny rocks, only to be told that every geologist

in the west has been in and covered every square inch.

If you have ever been to the Canyon of Gold, you also will know the truth that no human being will ever see every square inch of the canyon, let alone know its content.

Life is too short for that. To date, I am third in the seniority list of mining occupants of the canyon. At one time, I had consolidated all three of

our claims and had made one of the largest fortunes in the canyon since Buffalo Bill.

Had Buffalo Bill or any of us known it all, I'm sure things would have been much different. Considering that the known list of elements, to date, is roughly 1,000, and 50 new ones are added each year. Prior searches for free gold or silver are as antiquated as are these words you now read.

The Gold I sought was freedom from a sick society and a polluted world. I found it and for years enjoyed this desert world as most have never seen it since the original inhabitants vanished.

ORACLE HISTORIAN 1985

Article on the Iron Door Mine,
written for the Oracle Historian, 1985.

The Iron Door Mine Movie

Until *"Star Wars,"* the *"The Mine with the Iron Door"* was the first major motion picture re-done four times with the same subject matter.

Twice called the *"Mine with the Iron Door,"* the film was then produced as the *"Secret of Treasure Mountain,"* and then as *"McKenna's Gold."*

In 1924, the film *"The Mine with the Iron Door"* was proclaimed Movie of the Year by *"Variety"* magazine. In the 1930s, it was called the *"Riddle of the Rockies."*

All-star casts were in every one of the so-called romantic fictions films. Although they were fiction there is, and was, real substance that powered this gigantic saga– GOLD.

The film was re-made four times over the next six decades.

In 1936, the film was re-shot in Hollywood under the same name. Both were partial re-writes.

One version was titled *"The Secret of Treasure Mountain"* in 1955.

In 1968, it was released under the title *"McKenna's Gold."* This version was filmed in Canyon de Chey. The *"McKenna's Gold"* version hints towards another of Tucson's historical characters, Frontier Fremont, one of the McKenna's kin.

The Indian attack in the movie may have been part of the Kennedy Israel Massacre that took place in the Canyon of Gold in 1870.

The entire story will never be known, but will include some of this countries' most prominent and historical names.

A mine of such fabulous richness is Tucson's heritage.

"The Mine with the Iron Door" is not only the first movie filmed in Sonora, but is also an adventure ride at the Old Tucson movie location, plus the restaurant at the top of Mt. Lemmon Ski Lift named The Iron Door Mine Restaurant.

The Victorio Peak Treasure

Mariano Samaniego's descendants are tied into the WORLD'S LARGEST LAND TREASURE. Samaniego owned the Ranch property in the Santa Catalina Mountains where I lived. It is believed the treasures were moved to another location outside of the Catalinas.

Over 100 tons of gold, along with jewels and other precious items, are buried in Victorio Peak.

I met with Napoleon Samaniego and held one of the swords recovered from the treasure. Benny Samaniego was one of three people known to have seen the treasure at Victorio Peak. Back in 1976, "Rolling Stone" magazine did a feature on Victorio Peak and the treasure.

As with any such item as gold, there is very little documented evidence, many horrendous acts have occurred over this powerful and rare commodity.

Twenty-seven human skeletons were found tied to poles in the caverns at Victorio Peak along with many more in side chambers thought to be slaves that worked the mines.

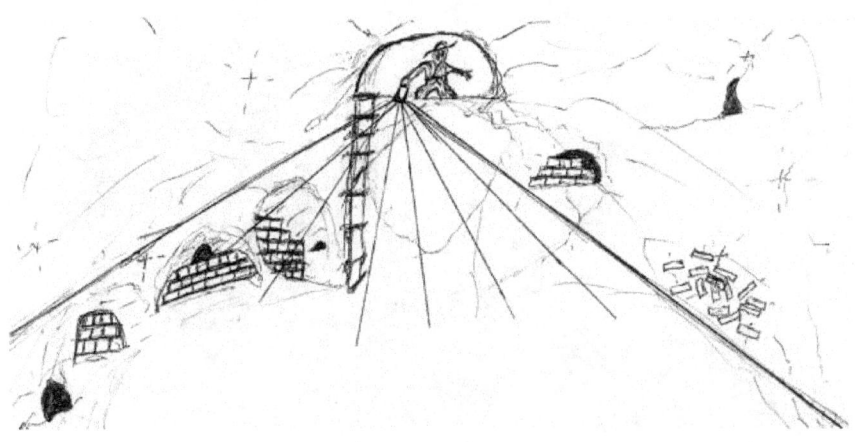

Is the Iron Door treasure in Victorio Peak?

Doc Noss' grandson Jerry Cheatham (left) digging in the Santa Catalina Mountains. Doc Noss discovered the treasure in Victorio Peak and was murdered over it.

William F. Cody

One person who reaped a fortune from the Canyon of Gold was the world famous entertainer William Frederick "Buffalo Bill" Cody– the largest icon of the 19th century. He had more guns, saddles, and pictures than any king or potentate of the century!

In fact, old Bill was the first "comic book super hero," thanks to the author Ned Buntline and his fictional dime novels about the Wild West and Cody. It was said that Cody retired in Oracle, cutting his hair and living out of the lime light of fame before his death in 1917.

Cody even worked the mines himself. Author Dan Russell said in his book that in 1903, after six months of drilling, Cody had hit the fabulous "Mine with the Iron Door vein."

After the famous vein of the Mine with the Iron Door was struck, 200 families worked on it until 1911.

William Frederick "Buffalo Bill" Cody. Photo courtesy of Buffalo Bill Museum and Grave, Golden Colorado.

Reports say that the ore from the mills was so rich the banks bought it straight from the mill– requiring no smelting.

The mines produced for eight years until the nephew of Cody's partner (Col. Dyers) fired everyone.

However, some power sources have changed history and claim the old scout lost a fortune – a scandalous charge that is nothing more than political geology.

Although the claims are that Cody lost between $300,000 and $500,000, he actually sold 361,000 shares of stock from $1 to $12 a share (see Shareholder chart on the following page).

Funny how things change when money is involved.

No records of production are known, but it would surely change the claims that discredit Cody and Arizona's reputation. But, I have personally taken samples from far back in the mountains where there is a solid wall of silver and gold at the end of the tunnel. It is now caved in and hidden forever!

JANUARY 5, 1914.

W. F. Cody	415,610
D.B. Dyer Estate	258,870
N.H.Getchell	30
F.M.Hartman	30
Mrs.W.F.Cody	4,200
Lewis H. Baker	25,600
Mrs. May Cody Decker	450
L. E. Decker	300
F. H. Garlow	750
Mrs. Irene Cody Garlow	300
Mrs. Julia Goodman	300
E. J. Ewing	30
William Cody Boal	240
Fred'k H. Garlow,Jr.	300
Jane C. Garlow	300
J.Frank Cody	2,300
Mrs. J. Frank Cody	100
A. J. Cody	200
J. H. A. Beattie	200
Maud Mary Blackwell	300
Beatrice Davies	100
Sandy McVean	1,000
Ellen Francis Cody	1,400
Louise McDonald	100
Sarah Blair	100
C. I. Goulder	300
V. C. Goulder	300
Harry Corte	100
Dora Altwater	400
Jennie Love	200
E. Louise Friendsleip	100
F. G. Brock	100
L. W. Getchell	300
Barney Link	4,500
	719,410
Treasury	780,590
Total	1,500,000

List of shareholders of the Cody-Dyer Arizona Mining & Milling Company, January 5, 1914. The individual ownership of each totals 1,500,000 shares of stock owned.

56

A report by E.J. Ewing, Col. Dyer's nephew who took over management of the mine, claims no minerals were ever present. But, he spent his whole life there mining an abundance of Tungsten. The mineral Tungsten is associated with gold in these deposits.

Later on, less than 10 miles from Cody's claims, would become the United States largest UNDERGROUND gold producing mine at San Manuel. The town of San Manuel would be built for the mine workers.

Before we go much further, please in the future, refrain from saying "HOW I FELT." In many publications, I read how "Cody felt." That is not possible.

No one knows the extremes of this harsh desert, let alone before civilization, or how either of us felt. Sorry, but, you had to be there. You are lucky you weren't at the time. It was a living hell.

Still, the inner Canyon of Gold is void of mankind and dangerous to the novice hiker. Tread lightly!!!

The inner Canyon of Gold.

Like the song says, "even now the canyon stands defiant like a monolithic giant beckoning to all that wants its gold."

Most tales about William Cody miss the man and his accomplishments. Cody had an educational exhibit that brought the Wild West to the East and as far as Europe. But, he shunned using the word *"show."* Yet, he was forced to become a "showman" in order to survive.

At one time, Cody had a slavery exhibit with seven train cars of black actors to show the cruelty of slavery and the many talents of the African Americans. He stated they were very good musicians and excellent acrobats and dancers. The show, though, lasted only a few months. Cody was anti-slavery. In fact, his father suffered a knife wound during an anti-slavery speech and died from the wound two years later. Also, he strongly believed in women's right to vote.

As an old scout for the Army, Cody started the Boy and Girl Scouts. But, Robert Baden-Powell got the credit when he put the uniform on and really developed it in to the great state it is today. Cody brought the wild animals from the west and taught his little scouts how to survive in the new frontier.

In 1980, I had researchers at $100 an hour combing history, but did not find out until 1995 that Buffalo Bill was involved. Dead men tell no tales.

Code.

Colonel Cody--------Govenor	Lewis--------Charlestown
J. Frank Cody-----Buckskin	Humming Bird-Halifax
H. L. Merritt-----Broncho	Apache Girl--Havana
L. H. Baker--------General	Dolphin------Kingston
Barney Link--------Poster	Tom Cat------Lima
Hartman-----------Pueblo	Mischief-----Lisbon
Ewing------------Idaho	Careless-----Montreal
Chas. Brajavich-----Pony	Alto---------Houston
P.P.Ladd----------Missouri	Senator------Antonio
J.P.Sebring---------Dragoon	
Courtney De Kalb----Brazil	
Smith	So. Belle Mines-------Beauty

(Mining Claims)

Swastika-----------Dakota	Campo Bonito Mines----Royal
Aurora-----------Montana	American Flag Mine----Eureka
Poso Bueno--------Washington	Mill----------------Magnet
Summer Home-------Oregon	Mine----------------Electric
Golden Thistle------Utah	Railroad------------Tram
Juniper-----------Colorado	Gold----------------Stella
Live Oak----------Texas	Silver--------------Mary
Copper Glance------Oklahoma	Lead----------------Eliza
Summit-----------Iowa	Copper--------------Janet
Pure Gold---------Arkansas	Scheelite-----------Grace
El Plomo----------Louisiana	Assay---------------Bromium
Detroit-----------Mississippi	Ores----------------Radium
Omaha-----------Alabama	Option--------------Uranium
Mogul#1----------Georgia	Stock---------------Vanadium
Mogul #2----------Florida	Shares--------------Tantalum
Sulphide----------Carolina	Certificate(s)-------Iridium
Carbonate---------Virginia	Stock Book----------Barium
Merrill-----------Maryland	Honey---------------Tellurium
Ora Fina----------Delaware	Dollars-------------Strontium
Conglomerate------Jersey	1-------------------Calcium
Scheelite---------York	2-------------------Lanthanum
Rocker-----------Maine	3-------------------Niobium
Maudlin----------Vermont	4-------------------Molybdenum
Paga Ora---------Ohio	5-------------------Glucinum
Pirate-----------Indiana	6-------------------Thorium
Leyner-----------Michigan	7-------------------Cadmium
Gold Mill--------Illinois	8-------------------Aluminum
Don Pedro--------Wisconsin	9-------------------Cerium
Fresnol----------Hampshire	10------------------Chromium
Black Hat--------Massachusetts	25------------------Didymium
Alexander--------Island	50------------------Corundum
Dane------------Kentucky	75------------------Electrum
Gideon----------Minnesota	100-----------------Gypsum
Pinchot---------California	1000----------------Yttrium
Emily-----------Mexico	Concentrates--------Fluorite
Morning Star------Olympia	Tunnel--------------Franklinite
Happy Thot-------Spokane	Cross-cut-----------Graphite
General Hancock----Baltimore	Drift---------------Hematite
Old Bug---------Boston	Up-Raise------------Hepatite
Southern Belle-----Gibraltar	Winze---------------Ilmenite
	Shaft---------------Pyrite
	Open-Cut------------Tantalite
	Tons----------------Quartzite

Secret codes that were telegraphed

between Cody and the mines.

60

Captain Burgess and Cody

Captain John D. Burgess was Cody's friend and mining partner. He lived across the street from the present-day Tucson Museum of Art in downtown Tucson.

Similar in features, Burgess was sometimes mistaken for Cody. His daughter, Little Maudi, cared for both of them. The Maudina mine was named for her. She was married to University of Arizona geologist professor Thomas.

Burgess was known to have built extensive roads in the inner Canyon of the Santa Catalina mountains at the turn of the century. I believe he actually covered over a large part of the Lost City for one of two reasons– first to preserve or to destroy the area– so that mining activities could continue. Burgess and Tucson Sheriff Robert Leatherwood were both involved in the hunt for Geronimo with serious mining interest to protect.

From the Director of the Buffalo Bill Museum & Grave

By Steve Friesen (Scout's Dispatch, Fall 2010)

I just came back from a very interesting trip to Buffalo Bill's mines in Oracle, Arizona. Bill Carle, who runs the Pahaska Tepee gift shop, and I have been talking for years about such a trip.

I finally decided we had waited long enough and we high-tailed it for southern Arizona. It was a great time. Flint Carter, Buffalo Bill's biggest fan in Arizona and a one-man dynamo, took us on rough dirt roads up to the Campo Bonito and High Jinks mine sites. We saw wonderful specimens of what Flint calls Cody Stone– chunks of quartz veined with gold and silver from Buffalo Bill's mines. And we got copies of several hundred archival materials, including correspondence from Cody, relating to the mines' operation.

One thing that became very clear during our visit was the strong connection between Oracle and Johnny Baker, the founder of our museum. Not only was Baker one of the largest investors in Cody's mining ventures, he spent many winters in Oracle. Nearly every fall after the Buffalo Bill Memorial Museum closed for the winter, Baker and his wife Olive headed south to Oracle.

There, in an impressive stone house perched on a ridge at the High Jinks mine, the Bakers enjoyed a view of the Santa Catalina Mountains with the San Pedro river valley at their feet (not unlike the Museum's view of the Rockies with Clear Creek Canyon below). After Johnny died in 1931, Olive continued to winter at the High Jinks until around 1945.

Why did the Bakers keep returning to Oracle? And just what did Buffalo Bill find in his Arizona mines? There is a lot more information about Buffalo Bill's connections to Arizona waiting to be uncovered.

Once I plow through all of the archival material we gathered I hope to know whether Buffalo Bill lost his shirt in Arizona, as most historians have believed, or made a small fortune that was lost in ventures elsewhere, as Flint believes.

Now that's my kind of mining; let the hunt begin!

The Issue with Gold

"Gold does not breed cooperation."

Geronimo had once said, "We do not care for the land, for we have much, but what of the YELLOW IRON???"

How long has this been going on? Even today, people are told it is chalcopyrite and copper. What they are not told is that better than half of the world's gold production comes from chalcopyrite. None of nature's ores are 100% pure. That is why it is refined.

In the past, the copper mines were actually gold and silver mines, with copper being the greatest percentage of ore extracted. Also, platinum, palladium, rare earths, and other elements are found in the ore deposits.

Until electricity, copper was a problem to smelt and of little use. With the advent of electricity, the demand for copper was greater than that of gold.

Gold comes in sulfides, chlorides, oxides, tellurides, and zeolites, Although, mostly studied, there will be many new things in the future.

This will probably finally get me the bullet they said they would not waste on me: there have been many times that my life has been threatened over precious metals and certain information.

When I had the Player's Pub Bar in Tucson, a scary looking guy came over to me and said, "You know, while you are talking, you are just a drugged up drunk. But, you could be a problem if you started writing this down" So, I asked him if I could borrow his pen.

Here's how it works– and the American public is being robbed. All major mining in the U.S. is based out of Canada. That's the reason we cannot make another country come back and clean up the environmental disasters that occur during the theft of our resources.

The majority of most of the rare and valuable elements require specialty smelting and will not be recovered by firing alone. These become REJECTS and are sold to certain foreign entities who recover the platinates, rare earths, and the real values of the ore.

Foreign interest controls the commercial world with metals as the forerunner. This is as old as man himself and has been no stranger to cruelty for control.

As the news articles state, the Church has had nothing to do with the mining. The Spanish military dealt with mining and the slaves.

In the book, TREASURES OF THE SANTA CATALINA MOUNTAINS, four generations of Escalante's are profiled who were in the area who controlled the mines. This is the reason the Mine with the Iron Door has been also called the Lost Escalante Mine. But, in a situation where great wealth is involved there are no records and no directions to a fortune. An avid reader should also read the book TREASURE OF THE SIERRA MADRES. It's very different than the movie we all loved.

Humphrey Bogart played up the crazy part, but the book portrays how crazy the entire world was about the yellow metal and the lengths they would go to for it.

Four generations of Indians– Mangus Colorado, NaNa, Victorio and Geronimo– controlled the only water source on "the trail of the dead" and they captured many wagons loaded with precious metals and stored them underground in lava tubes.

One theory says President Kennedy was killed over this treasure. He reportedly visited the site six months before his assassination.

The Templars started the banking system in the 9th century partly because this noble metal is 19 times heavier than the average element meaning large sums had serious transportation problems. The only way to move heavy items before internal combustion was a person's back or an animal. One man alone could not carry a large sum of bullion/money.

The Lure of Gold

Most people are not informed about gold and the place it has held in history. In 1933, a federal law was passed that no one could possess more than four ounces of gold. There was a 10-year prison sentence for having any more. Only jewelers and dentists were exempt from this law.

Because of the ban, one local old man named Francis rolled a keg of dynamite out and set it off when the bull dozer headed his way. The remainder of the soles of his shoes are on display in the Florence museum.

After the turn of the century, on the backside of the Catalinas, 25 gold and silver miners were waiting for development when the ban hit. They were run off and the mines covered over.

Richard M. Nixon re-opened up the market again in the 1960s– decades after the ban.

Mining the Canyon's Claims

The tunnels we worked on in the Catalinas went to bed rock where there is usually an accumulation of gold. The desert has flash floods, so no large deposits occur as in areas where the constant flow builds sizeable deposits.

A truly magical happening occurred. When the gods were fighting in the sky one day, a thundering lightning bolt hit just across the stream from the mission. Steam was still coming out of the ground when we got there. The silver had melted into a solid metal glob!!

We took a pump and exposed the vein about 20 feet high and 15 feet wide.

One morning during the monsoon season, my Mexican friend showed up saying, "General, I have the troops, compressor, and dynamite." Wish I had a picture of four rough looking characters standing in a line of sorts.

We moved the compressor in the then empty wash and started drilling. The formation seemed like a soft fill instead of solid rock. The drill went in very easily, but was hard to get out.

I had never blasted before. We used a waterproof fuse and got the dynamite sticks a couple of feet down. We lit the fuse and ran. Five minutes later, we knew something was wrong.

Digging up the hot charge was no fun, especially the second time. In an instant, a storm came up and we barely got the compressor out of the now flooded stream. My Mexican buddy was spooked. He told me his brother lit the fireworks at the University of Arizona and had blown his hands off. The third time I said if this did not go off, I was leaving and would never again say the word gold.

The third time was a charm. We smelted the ore in a homemade kiln in the front yard. I still believe something is buried there– at least a good silver vein. Time has now covered it up. But, another good lightning bolt might reveal the location.

Climbing up the silver vein exposed by a bolt of lightning.

Sunglasses at the top of the photo to show the size of the discover silver vein in the Cañada del Oro.

Hidden inside the Mountain

When I arrived here, Burton Holly had told me that he rode horseback up the Canyon in the Santa Catalinas. He threw sticks of dynamite in the mine entrances to seal them and protect people from getting hurt in those ancient, unstable tunnels. He showed me a pile of crystals that he said came from a rich mine up stream that he found.

At one time, I had an emerald mine further up the Canyon. Beryllium ore which sometimes carries emeralds and makes many colors of stones. This was helidores– milky to clear crystals. But, like the Cody Stone, there was no market because of the rarity. So, I let the claim lapse.

Just east of the chicken coop was a small old foundation about ten by 12 feet. That spot has been over looked. Directly across the stream are two tunnels side by side with standard Spanish mining marked by two large boulders at the entrance.

(top photo) Two boulders marking the mine.

A sample of Cody Stone jewelry. (upper left) Cross donated to
the Lapidary Club for their Silver Anniversary.

The name Cody Stone was coined, by myself, in honor of the man who once owned it– Buffalo Bill Cody. William F. Cody owned the Campo Bonito mine outside of Oracle at the beginning of the 20th Century.

"I have seen the elephant!"

That was the cry of those lucky enough to have found gold! This adventure of a lifetime can be shared today in the "New Gold Rush" – jewelry grade "all natural" gold and silver in quartz.

Little does the average person know the value of jewelry grade 100% natural gold and silver in quartz. Apparently, the World Gold Council and Silver Institute did not either, as they stated so when I called them.

Buffalo Bill Cody made jewelry out of the extremely rich ore, found in the northern mountains of the Catalinas. Cody had pieces of this jewelry placed in jeweler Dixon's store front for all to see. He was aware the value of the rock that was first popularized in the 1850s by Tiffany's during the

California Gold Rush of 1848-49.

This little-known fact (because none of it exists anymore): 100% natural gold and silver is the most expensive in the world fetching more than refined bullion!

Empires have fallen over this noble metal and the history is almost nonexistent due to the power it holds over the world, with secrecy– a must if one was to survive.

Only one major source of jewelry grade exists in the U.S. from California and is sold through the Alaskan mint. As one of my friend says, "you can't get it anywhere else, and if you have to ask the price, you can't afford it."

Cody Stone is displayed in 14 museums worldwide, including the Mining Hall of Fame and the Gem Institute of America. It is the only specimen of jewelry grade silver in the Gem Institutes' collections. It is used in educational programs.

Only a few pounds of this material has been recovered with 450 pieces of jewelry being produced to date with various artists producing the jewelry.

In 1996, a New York appraisal of a piece of jewelry with an artists' stamp starts at a minimum of $600 in value. Cody Stone sells for $5 a carat for silver and $25 a carat for gold. Each stone is different and grading varies by the stone.

A Cody Stone exhibit on display at the Scouts Rest Ranch, in North Platte, Nebraska.

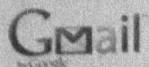

your Cody stone donation
2 messages

Terri Ottaway <Terri.Ottaway@gia.edu>   Thu, Jul 30, 2015 at 4:01 PM
To: "flintcartergold@gmail.com" <flintcartergold@gmail.com>

Dear Flint,

It was a pleasure to speak with you this morning and I'm glad to have a chance to describe how the pieces you donated of Cody Stone and the jewelry are being used by GIA.

We have over 300 students taking courses in Gemology, Jewelry Design and Jewelry Manufacturing Arts here on our Carlsbad campus. Our Education department has regular teaching sets of gems and minerals and they also select interesting pieces from the Museum's collection to take into the classrooms. The Museum pieces are of much higher quality and some have good stories associated with them giving our Carlsbad students an extra bonus. Your specimens of silver-quartz, catalog #'s 38585 (82.60 g) and 38586 (87.20 g) and jewelry # 38587 and 38588, are taken to the classrooms when the students are learning about the precious metals used in jewelry making. The fact these specimens are from the southwest and associated with the legends of Buffalo Bill makes them all the more fun to show.

Our Jr. Gemology program, for school children in grade 4, is currently getting revamped. Once they have a more secure storage for their rocks and minerals I may give the instructors one of the Cody stones to use in their daily program.

I really appreciate your generous gift of this material and our Library is delighted with the books and CDs.

Keep up the good work in preserving the history of the southwest and the characters that make it so wonderful.

With kindest regards,

Terri

Terri L. Ottaway
Curator, GIA Museum
Gemological Institute of America (GIA)

https://mail.google.com/mail/u/0/?ui=2&ik=d096bb873b&view=pt&search=inbox&th=14...   7/30/2015

Letter from the Gem Institute of America to Flint Carter for the Cody Stone donation to the Institute.

These pieces of Cody Stone are fabricated by Michael Garcia
(Na Na Ping).

Photo courtesy of Balfour Walker.

Cody Stone jewelry.

The *Iron Door Mine* legend is the west's largest gold legend. Four major motion pictures have been released over six decades that portray this golden saga.

Recent discovery of *jewelry grade* silver and gold ores have breathed new life into the century-old giant of the Canyon of Gold. Millions of dollars worth of silver in white quartz, a little known collector's item, was first discovered, and then gold in white quartz was found.

Arizona Daily Star, Feb. 2000:
"Buffalo Bill's Cody Jewelry Lost Mine Stuff of Legends."

Shane McClure of the *Gem Institute of America* said "chemical analysis revealed the presence of a small amount of silver" "It looks like some of this material will cut attractive cabochous"

Janna Cuccio of *Tiffany & Co.*, New York said in 1996 "I have never seen silver in quartz before, and as a gemologist I certainly appreciate the stone and it's history."

Charlotte Lewis of the *House of Onyx* said in 1996 "I do appreciate the sample that you sent and have prepared a display to be placed in our Mineral & Fossil Hall with the certificate you sent." "since there is such a rich history behind this mine and its products."

The Executive Director of the *Tucson Gem & Mineral Show*, held at the Convention Center, said in 1995 "We feel it was of great interest to visitors to the show as both a mineralogical and historic exhibit. We hope you will be able to return again in 1996."

In 1997 Robert Weldon of *Jewelers Circular Keystone* said "The pictures I took of your silver-in-quartz items turned out great! It will make an interesting gem note."

One million dollars worth of uncut Cody Stone was donated to the *Great American Wild West Show* in 1998. Don and Sharon Endsley, the producers, said "working together to combine our efforts and projects (will, i.e.) bring the excitement and treasures of the old wild west to the world."

Overview:
Only four mines in the world produce the rare white quartz and gold, and only 1% of all material being white quartz.

The natural nobel metals in quartz is a new commodity that has lured the prospector for centuries. The jewelry grade being the rarest.

The cultural heritage with this particular deposit entails the west's largest icons, and offers a literary and film adventure for all to share. The forthcoming documentary promises to be a treasure for all.

Facts, legends, and a new place in history for the Cody Stone. The mystery mining company of the Santa Catalina's as known by prominent people and media.

Hard Lessons from the Mountain

In 1980, I had one claim at the mission. I expanded to 172 claims in the Santa Catalinas butting up against the adjoining, working Little Hills Mine.

Combining the two together, we sold them for $500,000,000 to an east coast firm. After 10 years of walking 20-plus miles one way, and pulling my own teeth, I had made $125,000,000 by getting 25% interest in the new mine.

This is when I got to fly over the Canyon in two different helicopters. The first was in a skeleton tail, like in M.A.S.H. the TV show. We landed on top of a hill where I had seen a tunnel. But, when trying to leave, the chopper would not start.

All the money in the world is worth nothing when you are in the remote Canyon of Gold. Later, we got a jet powered copter and I got an eagles eye view of the Canyon of Gold.

This is when victory becomes misadventure. As they say, the rug comes out from under you while you are standing on it. Little did I know that in this life it is best not to stick your head up or someone will likely try to take it off.

Ted DeGrazia had once told me, "Boy, you are reaching for that brass ring on the merry go round, but will find out it is in the nose of a bull."

My father had taught me a man is only as good as his word. Dad never broke his word. It was as strong as steel. What Dad did not tell me is that everyone is not like him.

Little did I know the history or think how cruelty the original inhabitants had been subjected. In some aspects, I am the lucky one. The seven fortunes IN WRITING did little but get me in debt.

Personally, at first, the only thing in this huge legend I thought might be possible is finding a rich mine. Little did I know this was the LARGEST LAND TREASURE IN THE WORLD with over 100 tons of gold and more.

Prospector Flint Carter standing in a mine tunnel
in the Catalina Mountains.

A good book on the treasure is A HUNDRED TONS OF GOLD
by David Leon Chandler. There are three new books called
GOLD HOUSE.

But, certain sources in the know say the Gold House is
untrue. One thing for sure is there is– or was– a vast
treasure in hidden New Mexico. And, there was a Canyon

The Reef of Rock in the distance from the cabin.

of Gold connection.

The stories are endless as any great amount of golden treasures justly earn.

For example, a friend in Pennsylvania sister worked for the Pottstown Guardian newspaper and wanted to do a story on me while in town with some of my cactus furniture and jewelry.

I said, fine, as long as you don't tell them I know where the treasure is hidden. They would be pulling my finger nails off, and I would not be able tell them a location.

Back in 1977, headlines were "Prospector Knows Location of Gold." Ever since most interviews have not turned out like was planned.

In this composition, I have the chance to tell my side of the story, one not included in the stories published for the populace.

The 1977 trip to Pottstown.

First Trip Looking for Lost City

Flint Carter with members of the Oracle Historical Society in 1978 looking for the Lost City in the Santa Catalina Mountains.

I n the early 1980s, I discovered my claim near two partial shacks and the Lost City of the Canyon of Gold. It was in 1978 when we first went in with the Oracle Historical Society. But, it took a couple more years to actually find the Lost City location.

The members of the 1978 expedition with the members of the
Oracle Historical Society.

Only two buildings were left standing. One was very old
with a tree growing in the door way. The cabins were a
couple miles from the city. They were in fair shape for
shelter, but not for luxury. One board tent that remained
was Cody's. This Canyon was paradise and the richest
mine on the mountain.

ORACLE HISTORICAL SOCIETY, Inc.
Box A, Oracle Arizona 85623

Re: A letter of introduction to Tom Carter:

I have met with Tom Carter and reviewed the information and material he has gathered concerning the Canada del Oro area. I believe that the structure and artifacts he has photographed and the material he has presented warrant serious further investigation.. We are planning an expedition to explore and hopefully document Mr. Carter's claims on Oct. 6-9, 1978 in the Reef of Rocks vicinity.

We believe that co-operation in investigation of historical and archeological sites is an important function of our historical sositey and welcome your aid in the endeavor.

Sincerely,

H. Tom Thompson
President

Letter from the Oracle Historical Society regarding the first trip looking for the Lost City in 1978.

E.O Stratton and the Cabin

One story mentions that Cody and his close friend, William Neil, took three expeditions in the Canyon looking for the rich mine with the iron door.

I believe Cody knew the location of the mine. Also, that he was a friend, and business partner, with the Stratton's who had come to the Catalinas in the 1850s.

Emerson Oliver Stratton first worked the east side of the Santa Catalina Mountains. He then moved to the west side and upper part of the Canyon del Oro.

The first road built up Mt. Lemmon was called the Great Stratton Highway. It went to my claim– not the top of the mountain. It was finished the year Cody died 1917.

With the number of people growing on the top of the mountain, the road was rerouted and extended seven more miles towards the top so supplies could reach the inhabitants of the new community of Summerhaven.

An interesting fact is that Emerson Oliver Stratton was the father of Edith Kitt who started the Arizona Pioneer Historical Society.

Edith was first to record the story of the prospectors who, in 1880, found the Lost City in the Santa Catalinas. They told her that they found the iron door rusted off its hinges.

Edith grew up around the mountain spot where my claims now lay. There is a picture of the Stratton's in front of the cabin that we salvaged in the book LOOK TO THE MOUNTAINS, by Suzanne Hensel, on page 15.

The Stratton's were at the forefront of mining in the West.

Winfield Scott Stratton had the Cripple Creek mines in Colorado and was the only one to come to the aid of famous Haw Tabor, by lending him enough to hang on to his best claim The Matchless.

Called the "Silver King," Haw donated the downtown Denver Post Office and Opera House. But, the Sherman

Silver Act of 1887 stopped buying four million ounces of silver which evidently broke him.

The price of silver never changed from $5.00 until the middle the next century. In his day, Haw built ice castles and a huge fortune.

But, he froze to death on the steps of one of his old banks. Later, his new younger wife, Baby Doe, froze to death at the Matchless.

That claim (which is now mine) was sold to the Wilsons by Stratton for $50,000 shortly after the road was opened. Later, another attorney named Francis Hartman acquired the claim.

An interesting fact is that the Hartman Homestake Mine in the Dakotas was the largest gold producer in the U.S.

It is surmised that the progress and development in the West at this time frame was just a hand full of players mainly connected to Europe and the industrial revolution.

Half of the collapsed Stratton cabin.

The now-Ten Downing Street cabin restored in 1995–
formerly the Stratton cabin.

The remaining boards of Cody's tent shack before campers burned it for firewood.

Every producing mine had a connected railroad line. In the late 1800s, a railroad line that went north out of Tucson to Mammoth.

It has all but vanished now, except for a few visible areas.

Flint Carter pointing out a remaining stone wall at the Lost City in the Santa Catalina Mountains after it was finally discovered in the 1980s near Mt. Lemmon. The ruins still exist today.

The property was listed on the Multiple Listing Service (MLS) in 2013 for $100,000,000. It was the most expensive Multiple Listing in the state that year, the agent from Long Realty told me.

Flint Carter at the cabin holding a poster of Buffalo Bill Cody.

After exploring the Ranch since the early 1970s, it seemed that chasing the color to its source would be the best move.

I moved up in the Canyon to the cabin in the early 1980s and spent many years rehabilitating and maintaining that structure as well.

A Sign-in Roster, placed in the cabin, gave hikers a chance to leave their comments and record their presence (see the upcoming One Park Place Sign-In Roster chapter to read those comments).

The One Park Place cabin during the late 1990s.

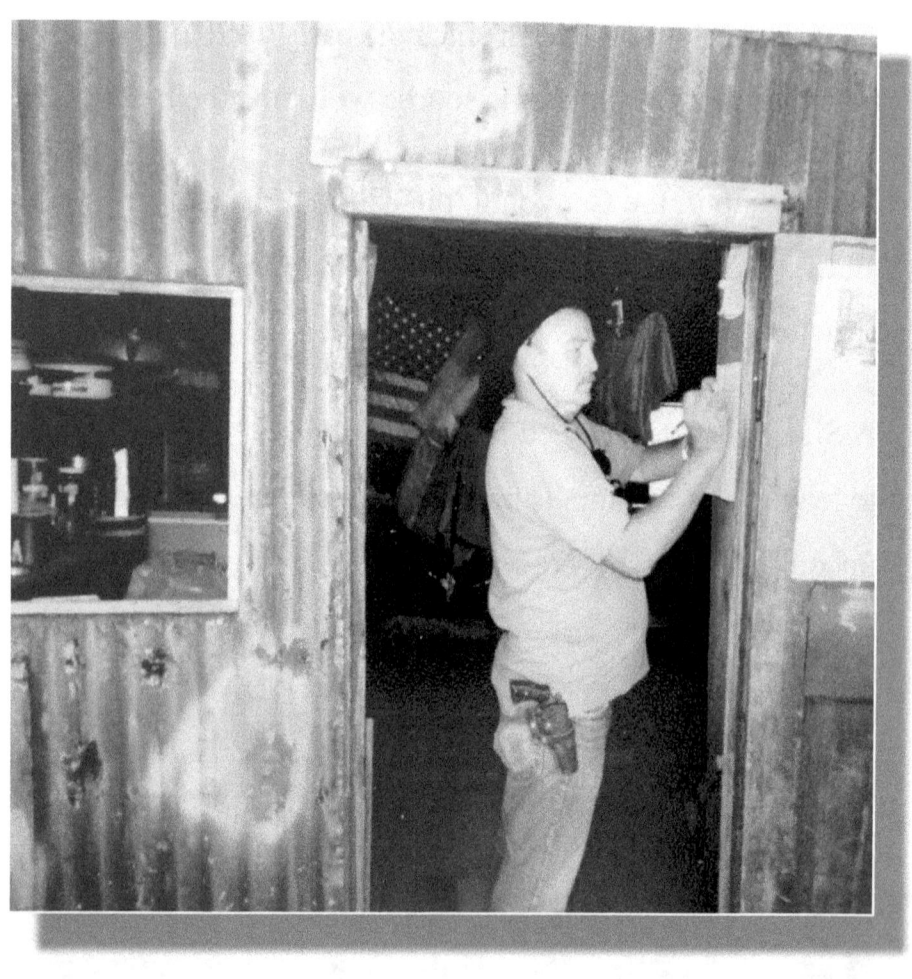

Flint Carter signing the roster in front of the One Park Place cabin in the Catalinas.

One Park Place Sign-In Roster

These are among the many comments left by hikers passing by the One Park Place cabin in the Santa Catalina Mountains near Mt. Lemmon/ Summerhaven. I have been managing, rebuilding and preserving this remote cabin for decades.

Visitors were encouraged to sign in and leave a comment.

Only comments from 1990-on are available. There may be misspelled or incorrect words as some handwriting was not legible.

Each comment is a story in itself.

Flint Carter in front of the One Park Place cabin.

Inside the One Park Place cabin about 1998.

Welcome to the "Canyon of Gold." There are very few sacred spots left in this world.

Since 1977 a sign-in roster has been provided and it is a special treat to see the names and comments of those who love nature.

A ballad, written by my friend Gary Holdcroft goes, "high upon a hill one summer, he saw the Canyon's gold uncovered, a treasure that no man could ever own!"

For more history on the area read the books: *The Mine with the Iron Door," "McKenna's Gold"* and the soon-to-be released *"Canyon of Gold."* It doesn't get any better than this!

These supplies are for emergency use!!! Please do not trash this beautiful piece of nature or the shelter from the storm.

Signed, The General ("Flint" Carter)

P.S. Keep bedding on wires because of mice. "Enjoy," and please refrain from making a mess.

Above, a look inside the One Park Place cabin. Below, Flint standing deep in the canyon.

The Macy's at the cabin.

Inside the One Park Place cabin in the Santa Catalinas.

1990

1/8/1990 The General & Rich

1/29/90 Just passin' thru - nice place, Good Luck! Chris Shaw (Mt. Lemmon Fire Dept.) Ted Adair (U of A Observatory)

2/27/90 Joseph Wilson

2/27/90 McGyver

2/27/90 Rich from the Windy City

2/27/90 The General

3/20/90 The General & Mr. Bob

3/24/90 Ricky C. Heast (spelling?)

3/24/90 Shawn, Mr. Bob & General

3/27-28/90 Mr. Bob, Shawn, Mike & General

4/9/90 Enjoy! John Cooney

The money bags wouldn't burn.

4/26/90 Troy G. Blackwell from Vegas & The General

5/20/90 Stuart Mendel (KA7FNQ Radio Op. Pima Co. Emergency Services (602) 747-1172) Guy (with Stuart)

5/30/90 Nice camp! (Oracle to Red Ridge Loop) Skip & Zenda, Tucson

7/20/90 Interesting - C.R. McLaughlin, Summerhaven Nice - D.L. McLaughlin, Summerhaven. Same here - T.R. McLaughlin, Summerhaven

7/20/90 Nice place, L. W. Auchard

8/9/90 "outrageous," Aaron and Linda

8/25/90 Michael Charles Montgomery, Tucson

9/21/1990 John & Mossie Lie (note: part of page is missing)

Flint at the One Park Place cabin in 1990 before it was redone.

1991

219/91 Paul Schmidt & David Walters

4110/91 Glad it's still here! Scott and Cynd

6/30/91 Thanks for the H20, Bob, Ken & Gonzo

7/20/91 Southern AZ Hiking Club

8/22-8/23/91 "Assessment Work" S.P. Littler (Steve)
Robert Ha (Bob)

9/22/91 Enjoyed the stay. George Mroczkowski 9/22/91
Enjoyed the country: beautiful, Alan Taylor

George Mroczkowski

Photo of George Mroczkowski

Author's Note: George Mroczkowski was president of the San Diego Treasure Hunters and the author of the book "The Professional Treasure Hunter." It took thirteen years to get George here, but when he did visit, he discovered an 1812 coin at the entrance of a blasted shut mine. He electronically searched the tunnels and found unnoticeable veins that were quite rich. He was a great man and friend.

The 1812 coin found by George Mroczkowski in 1991.

9/22/91 Keep Please, Robert Ha

9/22/91 Keep on, The General & Kathy

9/28/91 Dan & Hooter (The Loop)

10/6/91 The Maggie's Paw Group with Kamiack

10/6/91 Joel, Marci, rains (?)

10/26/91 Don Batta & Pete Yonsetto

A place where I'm not out of my tree (1992).

1992

4/11/92 Keep it just like it is, Ed Neubauer - Oracle

4/16/92 Lots of rain today! Scott & Cyn-d and the llamas

4/25/92 Jim Nekon

4/25/92 Ed Neubauer

4/28/92 Neil & Ben Finch

5/2192 Great Walter Watson

5/12/92 This time Linda couldn't make it. Aaron with Norma

5/16/92 Better 2nd time. Walter Watson

5/16/92 Jeff Arrowsmith

5/16/92 N.JOY ARIZONA. Bob Banghart

6/29/92 Lost Hiker's Search (successful), S.A.R.A., John Sims, searcher Greg Roy, searcher

9/18/92 Paul Hardy

9/18/92 Backpacking from Dan's Saddle to Oracle, Jason Ashbrook

9/19/92 Ian Whyte

9/26/92 Daryll, Larry Shipley

9/26/92 John, Medley

9/27/92 Jim Klein

10/3/92-2:45 pm Jim Roberts, Oracle

1019/92 Jim Thompson, Merle Watt, John Bonefas, Roger Sather, Don Fletcher

10/24/92 Robert Hall

1993

3/23/93 Thanks! Just in time for the rain. Peter McBride

5/8193 Great cabin! So AZ Hiking Club

7/25/93 SAHC (8 hikers)

8/4/93 Robert & Rom

7/8/93 Lin Fadden

7/8/93 Rob Cushman

8/18/93 Paul & Lisa

9/18/93 Catalina Cross-Country

10/12/93 Just passing by! Rich & Kate

10/22/93 Had to show her! Aaron (Jared) & Karen

late 93 or early 94? Make any new trails lately? Where are your morals? Do you really care about the mountain or do you only know how to recreate? What about the trash? It makes me want to puke. Southern Arizona Hiking Club.
(Author: "Everyone is expected to clean up after themselves.")

1994

5/12/94 Just passing thru. Put the flag right side up. Bruce & Brett Moore

5/14/94 Hey, we read the *Tucson Weekly* and I want to know what happened to Gladys' head? (*Tucson Weekly* Aug '93) Let me know (*Author's note: A friend of mine broke up with his girlfriend who was a hairdresser and the head was put on the shelf as a kind of freaky joke. It scared the B-Jesus out of most passerby's and was in a Tucson Weekly story about the cabin and the beauty of the area. Plus, Ghostly Gladys spending the nights and years and she is no dummy!*).

5/16/94 Hey! On leave from the military - Just kinda passin' through - Chris & Spencer

5/22/94 Hi! We just came down Oracle Ridge - beautiful! Peter & Joanne Knagge

5/29/94 Passed down on Red Ridge and going on up Oracle Ridge. Didn't need the amenities, but nice to know they're here. Les Reese & Brian Gross & Eric Thing

5/31/94 Down from Oracle Ridge to Catalina Camp & back. Cliff Holmes

6/20/94 Oiled your door hinge - still don't work. Cliff Holmes

7/10/94 Jim & Cheryl Welckle - Oracle Mark Vancas - San Manuel, 8 llamas: Transformer, Sundance, Matt, Tonka, DeMott, Badger, Farlow, Walter

7/30/94 Admired your well-stocked homestead - wondered how you got it all in here. We're camping at junction of Red Ridge and this trail to Dan's Saddle. Alice, Kim & Leanne Stone (15 mos.)

8/4/94 Trekkers from SaddleBrooke. 5 people

8/17/94 Just passing thru - nice find! Robert L. Coleman & Greg Corman, Tucson

8/17/94 Very impressive - Jessie, Ada, Jay Hoying (?), Ed Toth

9/13/94 Welcome to the "Canyon of Gold." There are very few sacred spots left in this world. Please refrain from making a mess and enjoy! Since 1977 a sign-in roster has been provided and it is a very special treat to see who signs and their comments.

Read the book THE MINE WITH THE IRON DOOR, MCKENNA'S GOLD and the soon-to-be-released CANYON OF GOLD for info on the past inhabitants of this beautiful valley.

A friend wrote a song about the Canyon of Gold: "High upon a hill one summer, he saw the Canyon's gold uncovered, a treasure that no man could ever own." The General & Jeff

Ed Toth

9/19/94 Three days of Paradise. The General, Ron Cappello
Ed Toth.

Flint Carter standing with Ed Toth.

Author's Note: Ed Toth was a white medicine man and practiced religiously. He had the kindest heart and had cured caner in one little girl at his ceremony.

We did a Chanupa ceremony which is an offering to the four directions of the wind. It was chillingly still and at the end of the offerings of tobacco and sage from nowhere came a strong gust that shook the trees and picked up my cowboy hat that got caught on my stampede string and just stayed 1½ feet above my head for at least a minute or two. Very strange.

In late 1980s, I had gone during a Halloween full moon to the cabin by myself and called out the ghosts. It was not a smart thing to do in the middle of the night. The window next to me opened and a strange shadow was two feet away. Immediately I grabbed the gun pointed and fired five times with no results. Then, I turned it toward myself it fired, just barely missed blowing my own head off! There has never been a white boy pray that hard until the sun came up.

For a couple years, I had told people how the shadow had

jagged edges in the shadowy moon light. After we opened the spirit horse trading post one day, Ed Toth hands me a hat box that had skull cap. A letter included said, "Tasia, son of great Charrawa war chief Cochise Edward Sands 5th Cavalry 1885 – it was the same layered turkey feathers that caused the jagged shadow I had seen at the cabin!!!!!!

Ed returned the skull cap to the Apaches. By the way, the term Apache actually refers to the 'marauding' street gangs in Paris during early 1800s. There is no mention of this being the natives' name until after the advent of foreigners.

It also was not the best gift for the Apache because Tasia was the white mans' police. Geronimo got all the fame, but, Niache, Cochise's second son, was Chief. Geronimo was a general. The only reason these Indians were not killed was because the two brothers could cut a deal. Upon surrender, Tasia was shipped to prison in Florida along, with the rest of the tribe.

Ed was the one who returned Tasia's War Bonnet (Cochise's son) to the Apache's at Fort Sill in Oklahoma. He took his own life over lawsuits about the bonnet.

9/27/94 A place in time, we spent a little time with God and his creations. Enjoy a peace of mind. "Great days." Tom, Bob, Tom

10/8/94 Robert Surma, Harry von Bergen. Thanks - Robbe Cain great spot – Freda Johnson (and one more)

10/21/94 Jim Thompson SAHC and Over-the-Hill Hikers.

View toward the Reef of Rock in the middle of the Catalinas.

1995

Returned again to be healed from society's mistakes. The General.

4/1/95 pump & blast, Jeff Petroski

4/30/95 Very nice! Kelly & Slim, Bisbee

4/30/95 Commanches - run for the hills

5/10/95 69: Peace! Big Trav & Wencemeister

5/11/95 Returned to do more work - peaceful today - lots of birds Singing Bob, the General, Mark

5/14/95 John Huntington Jim Huntington We took nothing but pictures, we left nothing but footprints! George F. Deming IV, Phoenix

5/16/95 Jim Officer & the General

5/16/95 Larry Bagley

5/26/95 "The Banker with Vision," Rob Stevens & the General

5/27/95 It's my birthday & it's great to be here again. Steve Adams

5/27/95 Had a great hike! Marlyn Cassler

5/27/95 Judy Cathey & Kevin Apland

6/9/95 Sue Herman & Hilda

6/11/95 What an amazing surprise! Pier Ingram

6/11/95 Natasha Korshak

6/15/95 A treasure RJR

6/?/95 Saturday – a wonderful place. Thanks for the ice pack, will replace soon. M.D.

6118/95 Beautiful place; just passing through. Plan to take more time next time. Thanks for the nice time. Sigmund Fensel & Kenneth (Staas) Coleman

6/24/95 Just passing through. Glad to see the place is still here. M. Brookshier

7/2/95 This must be of the kind of people I've dreamed of, NICE! AL from FLA

7/7/95 Tom & Larry from SaddleBrooke

7/16/95 Hope they never tear this one down Richard Kane & Beth Staats

7/18/95 Looks good! I've been coming thru here for 20 years. Gay Sutton

8/16/95 Polly Reynolds, Saddle Brooke Mary Murphy, SaddleBrooke George Skipp, Saddle Brooke Don Kirk, LaReserve, Oro Valley

8/25/95 Bob & Sandy Erickson, Tucson

10/1/95 Ramblers Hiking Club

10/21/95 Ed & Jannelle Emerling, Marti Elhin (?), Althea McClure

(sometime between 10/21/95 and 11/895) The long walk. Mark F. Evans, Georgia

11/8/95 We are tempted to take longer rest here! SAHC: Ursula Hess, Khristel Claanen, Claus Claanen, Del, Bonnie Huntley, Pat O'Donnell

11/30/95 The General & D. Goode (D Ranger)

12/1/95 Beautiful! Mary Bradley

12/1/95 Just tempted! Jimmy Jordan, Bisbee, AZ

12/1/95 This one's for you, Pappy Thanks for the door handle! The General

12/11/95 Been tempted! Jimmy Jordan, Bisbee, AZ

12/11/95 - 11 am. Arrived to let the heart roam free for a few hours in the Canyon of Gold. Be safe and God bless. Bobby Hall, Mary Bradley, Bisbee, AZ.

Melvin See

12/8/95 Melville See, Tucson

Mel See and Flint Carter in front of One Park Place.

Melville See was called the Princeton Hippie. He had degrees in Geology and Cinematography. Mel wrote a favorable report on the mine. He was Linda Eastman's first husband and when they divorced, she married Beatle Paul McCartney. While at the cabin, I asked him if he was Jo Jo in the Beatle's song. He made it clear he did not want to talk about it. About a year after Linda died, Mel took his own life.

Paul McCartney is helping to raise Heather, Linda and Mel's daughter. He was a great man and is missed dearly.

12/2/95 Doing a little prospecting and enjoying the scenery. Jim Pruden, Denver, CO & Tucson, AZ

12/8/95 Returned to a little bit of heaven, the day being a day of peacefulness. Looking for Santa - Bobby

12/8/95 Best wishes to all! The General

12/1/95 Yeeha! Door & tin on new cabin. Mr. Bob & The General

1996

2/3/96 Nice pencil. Jeff Baierlein here, hiking Northward into the snow & the peak of Mt. Lemmon. It's quite nice here, not raining any longer, although my shoulders are sore from backpacking. Glad to be here.

2/13/96 Can't imagine a better place to shut out the world of man, s'long as you don't mind sharing with ghosts. Beware the full moon. Alan Heyman, wanderer

3/13/96 There is a God. Thanks. Wayne Zespy

4/27/96 Wow!! What an unexpected & pleasant surprise! Thanks for the thought!! AZ Trail Volunteers

4/27/96 Bob M, USFS, Coronado

1997

?/97 "High upon a hill one summer he saw the Canyon's gold uncovered, a treasure no man could own." Gary H.

4/11-12/97 The Count of Catalina

4/13/97 Thanks, Flint - a beautiful place and a lot of hard work went in here. I'll see if I can get you what you want. Stephen Gilley

5/2/97 Enjoyed the Palace & left you some food. Troy, Hugh & Gloria

5/7/97 Halfway JEAM

5/15/97 Stopped on the way, Gail

5/17/97 What a great place to take a break. Been coming thru here for 25 years. Camped below by the creek. Left salt by the vortex for the Bigfoot. Gail

6/?/97 8 days out, so many more to go. Once again, this hollowed range a resting place for my wilderness soul.

Thank you General, for relief and respite. Sunshine & Susan, Shiela, MoShiela

6/18/97 3 guys with packs, Tues.

6/31/97 Place looking a lot better and beautiful as ever. Been about 5 years. Oscar. P.S. Thanks for the history lesson Sunshine

6/14/97 I love what you've done with the place. Sorry to say I just stopped in for a moment, but may take advantage at another time. Must keep pushing on. Alex

6/14/97-6/18/97 Down Red Ridge going to Oracle Ridge and out to Fire Sta. (We hope) SAHC

7/3/97 I left on my 46th b'day on July 1 from Finger Rock Trail but blood showed up in my urine so I went back out. Dr. gave me antibiotics for infection & said I could finish my hike. So, evening of July 1 started @ Mr. Lemmon. From Marshall Saddle to Sutherland Trail to La Canada del Oro where I got detoured somehow. Was going out Oracle Ridge but not if I don't get water first at the mines over the saddle. Onward & upward. I left some ziplocked chow including some turkey jerky. Phil Muir

7/4/97 This place is very nice. I cannot believe the total peace & solitude on the back of the Catalinas. So many people festering in the valley like maggots in a warm fleshy carcass, we devour anything in our paths, I hope there is a higher purpose to all of the destruction of nature, I am thankful for the serenity of the trails. Happy Independence Day. Shayne P.S. Thank you for the history note, it's nice to know that nature is appreciated.

7/6/97 Well, my soul feels cleansed of the filth from the city, I guess I can go back for another week. I borrowed your Reliance 5-gallon water container and left some untreated water in it. There is a little pool of water about 100 yds. downstream from the junction. Be kind, respect Mother Nature, and never reap what She has sown. Back country man Phil Muir. P.S. How about picking up some of this trashy metal, it does not blend with the landscape. It makes me want to puke!!!

7/10/97 Thursday Trekkers - Saddle Brooke Polly Reynolds

7/13/97 A very unique little oasis in the desert - never been anywhere like this in over 600 days in the field. Thanx for the human kindness & we'll be back for some grocery drops later, Joanne Wright & Russell Chamberlain. For all things, there is a season – Namaste General I had left the city, for its dirt & grime. Factory work, to make mountain time. Here I found love (B.T.) Sunshine What a long strange trip it's been G.D. This is the essence of true beauty. Shalene, my girl and I planned to go roam the DCO while it's still temperate. As nature would have it, monsoons built up and we scurried here for a little shelter. Upon entering we read the register and realized we had started seeing each other 2 months ago to the day here! Sunshine Your comments are treasure.

My pal, Raffiel Francis.

10/4/97 - 4 more days and I'm 50 - 27 years of Paradise.
The General This place is cool. Raffiel Francis from N.Y.C.

10/4/97 This is not an abandoned cabin. This is private. A
loved place appreciated by one and all, maintained and
built by hand. Let it be. For time. Balfour Walker

1998

4/11/98 Thank you for the snack for an always hungry hiker. Mark Morrison: Arizona Trail Hiker (Mexico ~Utah) Mommy, look at all the trees Mommy, look at all the little animals in those but here comes a cloud a very dark cloud what will happen do you suppose? Mommy where are all the trees? Mommy, where are all the little animals? Mommy, Mommy, where are you? Help save our Mother. We all make the world the way it is.

4/29/98 Thanks everybody for keeping the place tidy. Please remember to pack out your trash. Black bears roam here, & we hate to remove trash-dependent bears that have become aggressive to people. Enjoy! Forest Service

5/9/98 Great to have a home for the night. J.D., Wisconsin

5/16/98 Brief rest stop, back to Red Ridge. Back

6/9/98 D. High W. Borton The Santa Catalina Mts. are supposedly named by Padre Francisco Kino on the day of

Saint Catarina. This area, the North Canyon and Slope, where the principal paths of exploration by miners, woodcutters (for the large Mammoth, AZ smelter), and ranchers. A stamp mill and ore machine still exist in the drainages near here and Coronado Camp, mute testimony to hundreds of men and women who toiled in the wild southwestern wilderness after the turn of the century.

Gone are the days when strike news was expectantly waited for in Tucson and Mammoth. Nor do I think anyone got outrageously rich, though the Oracle mine still operates in what was once the "Ole Hat" Mining District. But before they left the miners cut and blasted the Oracle roads last nine miles to the village of Summerhaven.

Considered a heroic feat, the road was so narrow and treacherous that passage was controlled and traffic moved in one direction part of the day and the other direction the other part of the day, hence the name "Control Road." Still, this small dirt track provided the only non-stock or footpath access to the Catalinas and Summerhaven until 1952.

Most ranching outfits are long gone and the air no longer rings with the sound of blasting and the grind of mining machinery. Nature reigns now. slowly retaking the land that iron and steam reshaped. As you wander this range, leaving only footprints and memories, please remember those who came before. Sunshine Welcome to Catalina Camp leased by the Iron Door Mine Inc. We welcome you to enjoy this special part of nature and please respect it! Eat all you need but leave some for others who visit it! The sign-in roster is part of a new book called "The Canyon of Gold."

5/24/98 20 years and it just gets better! The General & Shawn S, Lynn Cisci

5/25/98 EUK Gail Sutton

5/24/98 Camped out through today a few hundred yards upstream from Catalina Camp which is down by the creek where the trails meet. Check your map. I've been hiking through here almost 30 years. This old shack was decrepit back then. Great restoration. Anyway, the far east fork of Canada del Oro was running quite well. Even a side canyon had water. Ladybugs were thick, almost a nuisance there were so many. Tucson may have hit 100 degrees today, so I know my hike from here to the sawmill will be sunny and warm.

5/29/98 Back again - Ahhh, another season in the CDO. It's good to see it's still so good. Today & tomorrow we restore Coronado Camp!! Sunshine

6/6/98 Mtn. biked from Oracle, down Red Ridge. I like this old cabin! Lee Blackwell

6/6/98 Rode w/Lee up #38 down Red Ridge back to Dan Saddle, Oracle Ridge. Just passing through. B. Barf

6/20/98 Orner Khan (Pakistan) Kersten Menzel (Germany)

6/27/98 Heading back up! Craig Gordon

6/22/98 Toni Laxague

6/28/98 Steve & Teresa Snider

7/21/98 Thursday trekked SaddleBrooke. Polly Reynolds

7/13/98 Is not our God so incredibly awesome - just look at all of this awesome beauty that He created. Praise God!! Sean Millhorn, Cheryl Hudgin. God is what life is about! There is NOTHING without Him!

7/18/98 Camping was great Royal Rangers - East Side Assembly of God

7/18/98 Joseph Sacco Danna Field

7/23/98 The Iron Door Mine, Inc. welcomes all travelers to our humble abode. You are invited to use what you need and leave what you can, for those who follow behind you. Please register your name for a new book being written called "The Canyon of Gold." Robert J. Tanin

8/7/98 Terry Metcalf, Orue Gilbert, Tash Lawrence

8/10/98 Lee & Mike and 3 dogs, Tucson

8/21/98 Dean McAlister, Tucson Bob LeJeune, Tucson

8/21/98 Hurricane Bohne & pals, Tucson 9/1198 Ricki Mensching, Tucson

9/1/98 Harry & Dorothy Wilhelmsen

9/1/98 Cathy Casey, Ft. Walton Beach, FL

9/1/98 Tosh Lawrence, Tucson

9/10/98 Wendy & Matt Scholtz Paul Weideman

9/12/98 Todd & Jamie Vlastnik

9/12/98 Brent Sneller, Grand Haven, MI

9/17/98 SaddleBrooke Hikers (9 in all)

9/17-18/98 Donald Miller

9/17-18/98 Fred Janz

9/20/98 Sarah & Michael

10/18/98 3 Smiths

12/24/98 Merry Xmas - by bicycle Dean Luger

12/26/98 Paul Leech Emanuele Souza, Torino (Italy)

1999

3/1/99 The General. A special prayer! "Cisco." Just great Harry Hower, Edgewater B. C. Great hideout Jeff Lainhart back in 1999 USFS trail crew Sunshine Thank you, this is great! I too hope that this historic place will always remain as it is in our heart's as home. Sincerely yours in the wilderness experience, "was hear" Joe, U.S. Forest Svc. SU.

5/2/99 Sunny, not too hot - just perfect - we left everything as we found it. Thanks! Jake & Sandrine, Anne Arbor & Laninon, France

5/29/99 A little warm, Christy Young

5/29/99 What a surprise to see a stable population out here - beautiful country - hard work! Gary, Leslie, Nathan & Daniel (and Kirby the smooth fox terrier)??? Welcome to the "Canyon of Gold." Please enjoy and respect! Your comments are appreciated and will be part of a historical documentary. Many books & movies portray this area's history: (AZ Hoof Trails _ Woods; Iron Door Mine - Wright; Oracle Speaks - Schifano) Enjoy, The General.

6/17/99 Dr. Flu just passed thru. Howdy to you!!??? Please remove trash from Catalina Camp. This is a beautiful area. Let's keep it that way! Sandy Sledge

7/6/99 Joe was here.

7/6/99 Adam Lockyer - Back Country Trail Crew

7/6/99 "yo tengo las mas grande verga del mundo." Hopi con (?) Jed Hammer Joseph Nettle

7/10/99 This is a great idea - thanks to everyone! "If the thunder don't get you, the lightning will." Jean Svadlenka, San Luis Obispo, CA

7/17/99 Thanks, General - This place is a real life-saver during the monsoon season! Got rained on for 24 hours straight, and a dry place to crash fit the bill nicely Edward Gray & Harley (the dog) (paw print) "May all your journeys be winding and treacherous, and lead to the most spectacular view." E.A. (condensed version) P.S. Jean S - Thanks for the tip, you are an awesome individual!

8/5/99 Dr. Flu again cruising thru. How do?

9/1/99 Creepy, but very historical and practical. I like it. Excellent idea and implementation. Definitely make the path of lesser resistance worthwhile. Charles A. Willert II KA, RE, Y Dieu et les Dames.

9/2/99 Cliffhangers: Cliff Holms, Pam Parry, Carol Smith, Margorie Peterson, Kathy Schultz, Susan Tucker, Gary Kern, Mel Copeland, Marleen McCall

9/14/99 "Stop stealin' our signs" Sunshine Mike USFS Trail Foreman - SCRD KJ was Here! Yogi was Here!??? unknown dates - sometime before

10/2/99 In one week it will be 21 years since I was last here. I hope it's not that long before I return (??) Pack it in... carry it out... help keep the place clean. May the gods of the mountain walk with you... Sure glad I came. It is wonderful here. I'll be back if God is willing, Oct 2, 1999.

Paul Albrecht, Sr. B.H.P. 20 years (???) ??? Not quite Hawaii but good enough. Robert, had a great day looking for gold. Found many samples. Now if I could only carry out the name. I'm back, thank God. Paul A. Albrecht, Sr. 20

10/2/99 I was here for pure enjoyment. Some time I will be back. God willing! Paul Albrecht

10/10/99 Hidee-Ho we still go. The General. TLPZ - Back after 21 years. Time moves on but beautiful memories never fade. TURONE Pahaska – Where's Gina?

10/19/99 Today I came with time to share the sun and mountains with friends that care. The beauty lye's here. Janice O. When a fire burns inside your heart, let it be the torch to lead the way. Gina V Thanks, Gina & General Pahaska

10/17/99 David Yadgorov Thank to people who take care of the place. It's wonderful!

10/17/99 Back again for more fun - for love of nature, Janice

10/17/99 Tyrone & The General with lovely Janice

11/13/99 SAHC hike 11/16/99 Pazy bien! Maxofur

12/29/99 Had fun climbing on the mountain. Glad for the rest and lunch at the cabin. It's beautiful. Sunshine Woodford

Inside the One Park Place cabin.

2000

(Kept since 1991) Will be in historical documentary called *"Canyon of Gold."*

1/1/00 We had heard about the shelter, but were afraid it would not have been Y2K compliant. Yet, to our relief, it was still standing (smiling face). The Arizona Trail has been treating us well since our arrival on Redington Road. We have seen numerous beautiful sites from Hutch's Pool to the top of Mt. Lemmon, and now this adorable cabin. We will take home to Washington D.C. not only memories of the beautiful scenery, but also the friendly personalities we met along the way. Happy trails. Phun Kel & Krapik Caminando en el "Red Ridge Trail" Oli el distingvido aroma del rroyo. Con colores de otona, disfrutando del invierno. De fa sombra haua (spelling?) ellado con sol cruzmos de un canon a otro. De noche nos convertiremos en investras sombras. Te deseo todo 10 mejo de esta vida. (names of 1/21/00 not readable)

2/13/00 Reminds me of my days up in the Wood River Valley of Alaska. Glad to see places like this still standing. Beautiful spot, I'll look forward to returning. Mark E. Miller, History Dept., U of A

3/7/00 Paradise Rieu & The General

3/16/00 Thanks a bunch for the water and cokes for three tired horseback riders. D. Reaser (spelling?)

3/24/00 Arizona hiker, Mexico, Oracle

3/26/00 Charley Davis, Santa Fe, NM

4/6/00 Back again, I love this place. Paul A. Albrecht, Sr.

4/6/00 Some ride. Archie (Tommy R.R.)

4/6/00 Paradise Dave again

4/8/00 Scott Duecker

4/8/00 Open area in Paradise, Shawn S. & Thomas J. Davey

4/14/00 AZT thru hiking and friends stopped by Rob, Sail, Ken & John

4/15-16/00 The General thanks the troops. A fire break has been started. Please be careful with fire.

4/16/00 Thomas Davey & Shawn S

4/16/00 Bryan back. Thanks for the patio. It was a nice treat.

4/19/2000 How sweet it is. The General

4/19/00 I love this place. Came with the General. Paul A. Albrecht, Sr. & Chewy

4/19/00 J. Ringo was here

4/25/00 Time is silver & blood is colored gold Esmeralda never will grow old Please be careful of fires!! The General

4/25/00 I'll never forget this place Paul A. Albrecht, Sr. Chewy

4/30/00 Movin' dirt Rich Athey & Dog Brown

4/30/00 Can you dig it. Steve Rusin

4/30/00 Thanks to all the folks who so generously help maintain this spot!! The General

5/5/00 Thanks General! A very special place. Paul Pineo - Tucson

5/71/00 Cool place, the skippster was here with her buddy Shiffty. Thanks, General You are a beautiful person! Semper Fi, John Dell

5/16/00 General, just happened to come upon your nice little retreat. Thanks for the generous hospitality. Stop into the Alpine ask for Don, Bones, or Beaker

5/24/00 What a great place. Paul A. Albrecht, Sr. Chewy

5/24/00 La vie da sante is here! The General, Darrel & Rich

5/25/00 Love the chandelier. Real class! Saddle Brooke F Troop. 8 hikers

5/27/00 Retreat is one that requires an attack. Great place, thanks, Bill Elder

5/27/00 Earl Tilley

5/28/00 Awesome to finally meet the General. He is putting me to work. Great place. Shayne Hall Nice place, too bad the oaks are doing bad. Hope we get some water. Pat, Happy Memorial Day - some veterans got what we served for -God bless America. The General

5/28/00 Worked a little, relaxed a lot, Steve Rusin

5/28/00 Mike Barvey & Agatha Beins

5/30/00 Wishing I was there now. Hoping its still as beautiful.

5/30/00 On my way to Oracle ridge I met with a group of very friendly folks. What a nice surprise! Thank you for the ice cold coke. Aldo Magri, Oro Valley

6/16/00 May everyone that passes through here find clarity in their journey. Rob

6/17/00 If you can read this, you are enjoying the serenity. Congrats. Marty Party Deanna Kim

6/17/00 We're here, but rain. Steve Russ & Mark Hanes

6/22/00 The General Its so cool up here! Paul A Albrecht, Sr. Chewy

6/24/00 What a way to go, Steve Rush

7/05/00 Luna & Blue rested here – thanks

7/5/00 Solar power works! The General

7/6/00 I'm closer to the gold Paul A. Albrecht, Sr. Chewy!

7/7/00 Thanks, MW

7/7/00 BJ 718 Ricki Mensching, Jim Hawnley, Teri Metcalf, Jim Martin

7/11/00 So close to the answer ... The General

7/11/00 What was the question? Steve

7/13/00 just stopped in passing to check it out. Kevin Stoltzfus, David Baker

7/26/00 "Sunshine" Mike Watson USFS Wilderness Tech. - Trails foreman – "Wherever the trails take us," David Baker

7/26/00 "eat drink and be merry" D.M. peace to all. J. Lohmier

8/3/00 Carrie, Steve Jones, Kathy Alison, Maricic Sperry & Donna Van Langerveld, Harry & Dorothy Wilhelmsen

8/11/00 An interesting bike trail!? Sean Davis Slayer

8/14/00 We got into a little trouble! This was a godsend. We ate canned tomatoes & corn, which we plan to replace. Thanks, Jamie

8/14/00 Phyliss. Same one above - Thanks

8/18/00 Some interesting trail the other way! Sam Davis

8/18/00 Cool place here. John Meh

8/21/00 It'd be a nicer spot if people took their trash. Wyatt & Stacee and the dog Mason

8/26/00 Audrey & Sally

9/2/00 Camped out here for a few days. Thanks to the General and all others who have kept up this place. Cleaned up a little. Next time will bring in a broom. The rivers flowing well. Gail

9/3/00 Stayed here for six days. Good rehab from civilization. Drank lots of stream water. Read a lot of Edmond Bordeauz Szekely. Changed my whole life around. Got baptized by the Angels of water, sunshine and air. Nice place! Mark Ocha Tucson Citizen P.S. All praise, honor, power & glory to the Earthly Mother of the Heavenly Father!

9/9/00-9am Rode our horses down from Red Ridge trail head to Oracle, AZ. Can't hardly believe this is all here and not vandalized. Left 4 extra batteries in case someone's flashlight is low. Tracie Clegg– can't believe after 2 years of wanting to see this place, that I am truly impressed.

What a great example of how life use to be. Excellent adventure!! Marney Fairbanks

9/10/00 - 4pm Had to take shelter here due to huge downpour. Was planning to go back Red Ridge trail. Too late. Nice place to shelter from the storm. The Wanders 2000

9/16-17/00 Welcome!!! life is sweet! Please close door on frig & cabin. Thanks, The General

9/16-17/00 Great weather, great view. Enjoyed my visit and shall return. Thanks Mother Nature and the General. Scott K. Williams P.S. Our thanks to the rest of the crew of the weekend's work. Thanks Mark and Steve. We put a good dent in it.

9/16-17/00 I came a looking for gold & all I can find are these damn 60 karat garnets. Steve Reisner Sunday

9/17/00 A nice breezy sunny day. Quite a treat finding this cabin. Thanks to Doug Kreutz & the *"Arizona Daily Star."* Mark & Kim

9/17/00 -10:30am Hiked from Red Ridge. Didn't know it could be driven. Nice, if people removed their trash. 10:35 heading back. Ron Wassnup

9/20/00 4:20pm Arrived after quite a hike down, can't wait to go back up! It's nice to see people leave this place in good shape. Take care. 420. A&B

9/24/00 hey, groovy, or something. James and Aaron

9/24/00 Thank to the General for emergency care package like I've never seen. Will be back & bring some supplies to leave and help out. Kent Loper

9/24/00 Thank you General. I feel so welcome. I'll be back. Thank you, God. Lynne Schultz

9/24/00 What a wonderful peaceful place to stop and rest. Thank you for sharing. Amy Gorrell

9/26/00 Nice hike down, not looking forward to going up! George Dudzic

9/26/00 Beautiful little treasure on the mountains. Be back some day. Jesus Monteil

9/27/00 S.A.H.C. "Neat place." Ralf Deason, Erika Hartz, CindyZ, Ann H, Earl Hartz, Ron Stirling

9/30/00 The perfect place to relax before starting back uphill John Carroll It's addictive! Linda Hey! You guys got chairs! Nice touch, Rian Clawsen

9/30/00 Arrived here - first visit. Came down Oracle Ridge trail. Nice to know so many are helping to preserve these little treasures. I don't plan on staying the night but wish we had time to - this is what it's all about – Bev & Robert Yorkin

10/14/00 Two crazy girls took their bikes on a hike up Oracle Ridge from American Flag on their way to Mexico. Thanks for the tuna and kidney beans. The Shiela Monsters

10/28 Camping overnight - Borrowed shovel - will return on our way out tomorrow. A little chilly today - saw some snow up on the highway. Thanks. Scott & Shelly

10/29/00 Hey guys awesome place! 3rd time here with my buddy Shifty and I'm sure we will be back. Take care. Skippy

2/10/00 Bitchin - sunshine - killer – pesto. Thank you

12/16/00 Great place (luv it here). Came with Chewy my friend my dog. Paul A. Albrecht, Sr. Chewy

12/16/00 Still keeping the faith - grinnin & winnin. Happy holidays to all. The General Feels like home, Wayne N.

12/24/00 Hi General, It's Shayne Hall stopping in to say hi. I was the one who was going to clean up your trees for burn control. I brought my father to see your place. He was a miner for over 20 years. Progress looks good on your mine. Take care. Shayne Hall P.S. The tree clean-up looks great!!!!

Flint Carter climbing down the old mine shaft.

2001

2/17-18/01 Enjoyed cabin stay. Kept warm by wood stove. Great cabin. Happy trails. C. Beaver

3/23/01 Hey General - Great job! – I'm Impressed! AZ Trail hiker/runner - Mexico to Utah. Day #10 & turned out be longer than planned. Good luck to all & walk softly. 95 MEGA 98 ADT DECA 01 AZT MEXUT Keep truckin' Hoosiers! Brian Start, Tucson, AZ

3/31/01 Home again. Wayne N, Maricopa, AZ

4/01/01 30 years ago I came back to the States from a foreign jungle. Guess it was April Fool's Day. What happened to this country?? Honesty, respect, decency, honor still exist here. A special "good bye" to Archie who passed away Friday. He was a good marine and our party pal! God bless!! The General

4/16/01 Remember, before the miners were here, there were others here, the Apache, the Tohono O'Odham, the Hohokam and many others before them. These were people who were, and are still, part of the land here. These mountains became their bodies, and their bodies became these mountains! They are still here watching us! They watch us Tree and Rock, us Bird and Squirrel, U.S. Fox and Coyote, us, Mountain Lion and Bear, us, Wind and Rain. Be careful and respectful with your actions here. What you do, does not go unnoticed by the Mountain. Hears Like Coyote

5/1/01 Rabbit Rabbit! AZT Mex-Utah Grizzly & Sio Ride Shake'n'Bake Blelvis

5/9/01 - Sunday Puff puff - AZ to Utah Pat & John

5/12 -13/01 I came to enjoy. To get away I like it. Chewy likes it too. God bless you, Mom. Paul A. Albrecht, ex-miner Chewy

5/12-13/01 Dug a little - rained - happy Mother's Day Mom ~ sure miss you, god bless. The General

5/13/01 - Sunday 7:30AM? "Happy Mom's Day" Just leaving, "General." Thanks for a great place to come and relax. Had one of my best adventures here. Thanks, ever. Hope to come back soon to visit & work! Perfect weather. Good luck and best wishes, Jim Hicks 30

5/26/01 Just passing through, John & Lisa (WI Sara)

5/27/01 a pipe dream come true. Jenna, Sam, Alison (KY, IN, OH)

5/30 - 5/31/01 Stopped by for a couple of days Todd, Heath & Drew

6/2/01 What a pleasant surprise - a place that isn't trashed! Way cool! John & Chris UA

6/9/01 - 1 0:50am Sue, Misty & Michella want to say this place is amazing! We came in horseback, we rode Canada del Oro from Charloux Gap from Catalina up to Summerhaven. On way down, we discovered the trail leading to this place. Our 3 horses & 2 dogs & the 3 of us appreciate the beauty of this place, and how well kept the trails are as well as the fact it hasn't been trashed. We did not take anything. Thanks! (Van Dorns)

6/15/01 Wow! What a step back in time! I feel privileged to be a guest. Thanx - this is one in a million - what an adventure! Mark & Theresa

6/16/01 The Synergy group from Casas Adobes Baptist Church was here. Awesome. Dasha

6/17/01 Sunshine & Friends

6/23/01 Hey great hike! Sarah & Julie

6/23/01 Came & saw the gold moon in honor of those past in mine.

6/24/01 Southern Arizona Hiking Club Deborah Mayer - Happy Solstice, Steve Bogart, Philip Davis, Bill Tifft, James Carachan, Bob Fabuzza

6/29/01 Dan Davis, Mike Hansom, Dave Collins, John Maloney, Cyn-D Turner & Scott McMullen, along with Rigg the Wonder Dog. "I wonder what I'm doing?" Fine day in Paradise. Great day

7/14/01 ("Tom's (34) B-Day Ride") Rode in on mountain bikes during a storm. Was sure glad to find shelter. Thanks! What a nice place to run into. Signed, Ed Timberman, Chad Cornelius, Tom Lawler

7/15/01 Hiked down Red Ridge on a whim. Missed Gladys. Thinking about heading back by Oracle Ridge, but losing my ambition in this peaceful place. Maybe I'll stay awhile ... Mikel

7/21/01 Heard about this place. Very refreshing. Very clean. Feel safe. Thanks for all everyone's efforts to keep it that way. Mary & Tony

7/24/01 Great place- thanks Mountain Bikers Dick Bogart and Jerry Quesoul

8/5/01 Not to alarm or discourage anyone but there is a little fury guest living here. Maybe stock this place with mouse traps.

9/8/01 Michael Mellor

9/8/01 Tony & Becky Mellor

9/21/01 Bobby Oppel

9/21/01 Gregg Warren

9/22/01 Rick & Cindy Gerhart

9/22/01 Margaret Walker

9/22-23/01 I have traveled all over the USA. Where are you now? Simply at peace. Dig a little, have some sun, enjoy the earth, below your feet. The world turns another day. Jim Royce e-. 7th Engineer Div., 2nd Battalion FSSG, Catalina Base

9/23/01 Thanks General for: the experience of mining, and busting throw solid ROCK! It was a grand experience. The cabin was nice! But the stars were better! Keep up the good work - people love you! Thanks, Hienz York

9/22-23/01 The world has changed since the 11th, pray for peace! Thanks to all that do not trash this little piece of paradise. Dad, see you in heaven, sure will miss you. Wonder if the people coming here know how much you done for them. God bless all. The General

10/20/01 Alan Spitz was here! I am a veteran (but old) obsessive hiker currently trying to hike out the last system trails in the Santa Catalinas if the weather holds. Previous to this I have completed all hiking trails in the Santa Ritas,

Zion National Park, Kendrick Mtn Wilderness, Kachina Peaks - Little Elder, Mundo(?) Mtn, Granite Mtn Basin, Superstitions, 4 Peaks, Mt. Baldy, Escudilla, Sierra, Salome, Saddle Mtn. - a long list plus the Arizona Trail (built sections!) N of here and about 300 mi square of the Prescott Nat! Forest S of Prescott. Hoping this weather holds (and Arizona had falls and winters that dry in 1996 and 1982 at least) I hopefully move on to the E part of Rincons, 5 trails at Sheep Bridge in the Maratzal, Castle Creek, and Cedar Birch wilderness, etc. Don't know why people move here then love it when it's cold, rainy or snowy. Something wrong here. Personally, I didn't live here until 2000 and I've seen too many yukky days. Hasta la vista baby gotta run.

10/21/01 All the comforts of home, plus rodent droppings and a gas mask. Incredulously, I spent last night here, camped on the floor, was visited by no ghosts other than a tiny white spectre with long tail and whiskers, and now I depart, longs full of fresh air again and high hopes for the avoidance of hanta virus, plague, and the like. Now, I know where to go in the event of mass bioterrorism (and I'm only half joking on that one.) Blisterfree, AT GA-ME 196 LT, CT '98, Pct Mex-Con '99-'01

10/19/01 (& '86!) Great place of quiet & solitude! Namaste I, Shanti Gina & Shawna

10/20/01 Heard about white gold. If there's any truth to the story we'll soon be attempting unassisted fly-bys, Steve R.

10/20/01 Here I am again busten' rock, half way there. To where I don't know! But havin' fun. Be back soon to do it again. Hienz York

10/20/01 About the mine, don't mind the company is fine, fall runs Aspen yellow, bed rock- silver, Cody stone, heavy equipment operator. From Argonan... Looking for blue turtles... Roybal

10/20/01 White powder gold (David Hudson check internet) The General The place looks alright. What a lovely thing a running stream can be. Jeremia Burnett

11/3/01 Didn't know this was here. I will have to make us of it in the future. Drew Milsom

11/5/01 - noon What a surprise! Nice to get in out of the rain. Perfect timing. Hiking the Red Ridge & Oracle Ridge look. Marigold Love A perfect retreat for relaxation & calm. A special place to find. Monique Kundrat

11/9/01 Stopped by - no one home. Maybe next time! Norma

11/19/01 A restful, but creepy place. First but not last time. Eric Christensen - University of Arizona Observatory.

11/24/01 Great day for a walk. No reason to stay here. Peter Lashen

12/22/01 Some snow, but not bad. Enjoy!

The original wall at the caved in mine where we found the 1812 Mexican coin in 1993.

Halfway there and hit the big boulder in 2002.

2002

1/9/02 SAHC Hank Scussel, Ralf Deason

1/20/02 Looking for cattle and lions, Chet Wold

1/23/02 AZ Trail hiker passing through. It snowed all day today. This place is a nice fest spot. Took a chance & stayed the night. Desert Dweller P.S. Borrowed some water, left some hot chocolate. "The highest treason, the meanest treason, is to deny the holiness of this small blue planet on which we journey through the cold void of space." - Edward Abbey

1/27/02 Red Ridge - Oracle Ridge - up, up & awaay! Mike L&Solo

2/02/02 A couple of bionaut hobos stopped buy on a blustery winder's day but nobody was home.

2/15/02 My first trip to the Canyon of Gold. Beautiful, Tim Blowers

2/15/02 What can I say Beautiful Left Martin "Tinus" (?) Sanchez

3/19/02 Traveling through on way from Mexico to Utah. Camped at Wild Cow Springs last night in the snow storm. Wish I had gone the two miles more to here. Thanks to all who keep this a nice place. Tony Rasch, Bozeman, MT

3/26/02 6 Mtn. Ladies, Jeanne Hartmann

3/28/02 - 2pm The Canyon of Gold is a wonderful Place. I too am thru– hiking the Arizona Trail– maybe I'll catch up to Tony. I doubt it though since I'm taking my time and enjoying the magical little places along the way, like this camp. Anyone who has the chance should check out the upper part of the Canada del Oro trail. The forest there has Douglas Fir trees that are large enough to remind me of home. Looks like rain but I'll take my chances up on the Oracle Ridge Trail. Later ... John Brinda, Bellingham, WA P.S. Thanks for the root beer! Nice place to rest for a bit. Thanks! Bob & Danny

3/30/02 Out hiking with 9-year old son and 2 of his friends. Fairly easy 5 miles down from fire station. 3 miles back up look a bit tougher. Had lunch enjoyed the rest stop. Paul, Jeff, Steve, Spencer

4/4/02 Came with the guys. Good bunch 2 flats. The General

4/4/02 Co-Captains Jim Hansen, Herb Bevans CPL, Keith M Green, Nick Kelly, John Philip, Paul Brown, Ben De Silva

4/8/02 - 1:30pm Stopped here while hiking the AZ Trail north. Wonderful spot. Thanks for the soda and water. Next time here, we will haul out trash. Thanks much. Bill Leightenheimer and Kathy Gish, Tucson, AZ

4/14/02 This is Paradise! Reminds me of Gilligan's Island ... where's Maryann? John Davisman, Madison, WI

4/20102 -10:22pm Wonderful spot, 4th time for me. Walking up with 2nd hip replacement from last year. Won't be last time here! Love it. Walter Watson

Flint hauling out boulders from the dig.

5/18/02 - 2pm Cycling Oracle Ridge - what a treat! Did some maintenance (now not so overgrown). Resting here to attempt climbing Red Ridge. We'll see how it goes. HOT. But I'm loving it. Nice work with the cabin. North side of Lemmon is the true wilderness. Scott Morris

5/24/02 Chuck Seal, Woodstock, Virginia

7/18/02 Forests reopened TODAY! Came down CDO – lots of trees but a beautiful ride. Slow & persistent showers have followed me all day. Now, back to Red Ridge. Great cabin! Scott Morris

8/3/02 1st time here was 65 (10 years old) Back then there was 4 cabins. This trip came with wife, Tracy, and Son, Cameron, 14 years old. Thanks, will be back. Rob Sheldon (?)

8/30102 Samaniego Red Ridge loop. No rain this time. Woo hoo! Beautiful ride & Dayl Scott & Alan Morris

8/31/02 Back again Gen. Here to work on the mine, about got stuck on the road but we made it. Be back next week. Heinz York Thanks Uncle General! It's beautiful here. I'll be back again. Charity I'm back I love it up here quiet, and peaceful. Next time Chewy will be here. Paul A. Albrecht

8/31/02 One more sweet Jesus thanks ever so much! What blessings! We try to preserve and protect. The General

9/11/02 - 1:50pm - 84 degrees Hiked down from Red Ridge Trail. Knew about this cabin, but almost turned back when I spotted a deer which led me here. Spend time in surrounds & reading "An African in Greenland." Hope people will continue to respect this place. Que te vaya bien! John Kristofl Just hiking through. Refreshing stream below! Neat cabin – takes you back in history. John Dukes & Shelly Lemon

9/15/02 - Sunday. Do I have to go home? No! Not now I just got here. "I will be back!" I love it! Lawanda Kay Meade. Love it here – nice and peaceful. When are you going to pave to road for my car? Be back with the truck. Richard Fuarc

9/15-16/02 Paradise – but damn mosquitoes – will be gone soon - a little closer to opening 1812 tunnel. Lots of dirt in those holes. Before long we may know or maybe never. The General

9/20/02 Let's get this mine in production. Greg Becken, AZ Mine Inspector

9/21/02 Up at the Catalina Camp with the General, chipping away at the rock. Daniel L. Dunhill, High Jinks Mine

9/21/02 Came back to work this mine, have some fun. Great place to get away. Mark Howes

9/21/02 It's really nice up here. Count your blessing. Paul A. Albrecht

9/21/02 Bye, bye boulder – onward to the answers. Thanks to all that have helped in the adventure. The General

9/29/02 C. Stubbs 37 J. Couto's A. Jones Spirit and Ryan. We were here in Oct 2002, 2 smoke more pot.

11/20/02 Midday – warm - 6200 ft. – filled with mining history. Magnificent Canada del Oro - General's story-telling is life-filling & should be repeated - taped. A soft wind caresses this enchanted place - Blessings, Nancy P. Masland.

Photo of Wilma Huggett (left) with Flint Carter.
We have had more fun than most.

11/20/02 Beautiful view & peaceful R.S. Milam What a
beautiful place so glad to be able to see this side of the
mountain, and heard all the history. Wilma Huggett

11/20/02 Here, with Wilma Huggett, Nancy & Shane. Great food great fun. God bless! The General

11/23/02 Ricky and Dixie Dog

11/23/02 Scott Casale

The interior of the Canyon of Gold

Heinz York (left) bustin' a boulder. He worked blisters on both hands, cut them and went back to work. Flint Carter, center.

11/23/02 Bye bye boulder!! The General wants help once again. I am here to brake rock. Lovin' every minit. Heinz York

11/23/02 Just checking the place out! Joy! Kelly and Mort

11/29/02 Be happy - we are Mark Howes, Jim Royce, Scott Casale, The General

12/8/02 Scott Casale, Paul Albrecht. A little more comfortable!! Please keep clean, The General

12/10/02 Scott Casale, I'm going home. I'll be back Paul A. Albrecht & Chewy Stained glass for you - please enjoy!!!

12/12/02 I enjoy it up here, Paul A. Albrecht

12/12/02 Praise the Lord and pass the peace! Happy holidays and hope for peace on earth

12/15/02 More muck need some luck. The General

12/15/02 Just came to dig the place! Fleming Richard

12/15/02 Oh boy! Chewy is going to be piss off but I'll will talk to him. Paul A. Albrecht

2003

2/1/03 I love it here. Paul A. Albrecht

2/1/03 Top of the world looking down my nose at the shitty city, Uncle Bob

2/1/03 Damn boulder tuff nut to crack. We lost 7 astronauts today. God bless their souls and spirit of adventure The General

2/2/03 Jerry Cheatham, Las Cruces, NM (Note: Jerry grandfather, Doc Noss, was the original finder of the Victorio Peak treasure).

2/2/03 Do you know Jerry's story of Victoria Peak (??) The General

2/1-2/03 Spent night rolled rock in morn this is God's country, Richard

2/2/03 Chadwick

2/3/03 M.P. & B.P. (insert drawing of heart with question mark inside it)

2/22/03 Kelli & Hill, Boston, MA

3/28/03 Time: Noon Thanks! "Giddy up!" Jimmy Coyote & horse "Sarge," Tucson, AZ

3/29/03 A & A Zeppetella, Tucson, AZ 4/3/03 Quirky little shack. Onward on AZ thru-hike. Li Brannfas, Grand Canyon, AZ

4/5/03 I am glad I came. Paul A. Albrecht, ex-copper miner

4/5/03 Hope all visitors enjoy this piece of heaven as much as we do! The General

4/5/03 Back again. Just for a few hours it's still worth the trip. Richard Foard

4/13/03 Thank you! for giving me the chance sorry. Chewy, Paul A. Albrecht

4/13/03 Mid-afternoon, the cabin - thanks for the experience of digging in the past - again - my 2nd time here - About 80 degrees sunny. James Hicks

There's a saying:
shake the hand that shook the hand of a hard rock miner.

4/13/03 Still diggin' this place. Richard Foard

4/27/03 Just like the guide described. Very nice. Arizona Trail Hikers: Jeff Rundquist, Darryl Sieker

4/29/03 Love this place. Living in style tonight. Really love the chandelier! Thanks for such a cool place. (insert picture of smiley face) Sue Thomas (Alb, Canada) - going to Utah!

5/7/03 Breakthrough day? We'll see next time. S. Rusin

5/7/03 Came to work but had a good time anyway, Tino

5/7/03 Came for work & pleasure, got both. Greta

5/7/03 Much - muck - muck is a good thing! Closer but no answers. Enjoy, The General

5/10/03 This was it, Ain't no shit. Nothin but blue skies from now on, Steve Rusin

Breaking into the tunnel. Hit it perfect!

5/10/03 Dreams come true We found it! Loree

5/11/03 I stopped by this morning, met Tino. Nice place! Wayne Zespy

5/11/03 John & Lisa - Almost made it. Met us at bottom of canyon. Tino

5/11/03 This is where the past and the future meet in one fantastic place full of memories and future possibilities. David & Tina Russell

5/10/03 Gold, gold, gold. Paul A. Albrecht

The entrance to the tunnel.

5/10/03 We found it! everything is possible in life if you look, Terra Dinsmore. We came we saw the foe We opened the hole, Richard Foard

5/10/03 The experience of a lifetime Make it all worthwhile Congrats, General Robert Thompson

5/10/03 We did it! Just like planned. The General

5/11/03 Beauty is a blessing that moves through time and hearts – true, one of beauty and heart. David Russell

5/11/03 Came with the Denmark Doc and his lovely wife, shared serenity. The General

5/14/03 Zipitty do da, The General, Greta from Switzerland and the rich man of Catalina

5/17/03 Blessed be! Proxy to Nature, no relation. Sara Culberson & Melody Albright

5/17/03 Cleared fire break. Please be careful with fires – a dry year. The General

Homeopathic doctor David Russell. With degrees in five countries, has two books on healthy living. The classical tradition in the art of healing. According to David, "Health is a living response to the wholeness of being. The natural ongoing life of body, mind and spirit."

5/24/03 Isaias Torres

5/24/03 Kurt Keller

5/24/03 Thanks William - beautiful! David

5/24/03 Javier Mora

5/24/03 l really like this place. Thank you, General. Paul A. Albrecht

5/24/03 It's coming together. Awesome. Thx. Robert Thompson

5/18/03 Great Trail! Andrew Oacks

5/18/03 Brian Lipscomb

5/18/03 Beautiful scenery. Great hiking. Great place to rest. Richard from L.V.

5/18/03 What a change in scenes. It's turning into a show place. Steve Rusin

5/18/03 We came, we saw, we cleared the camp so it can be forever more. Robert Thompson

5/18/03 Another beautiful day in Paradise. Tino

5/18/03 Vice P. was here, work Sat, Sunday. Look very good for next time for S Mor. Here for the thrill of it. Nice weekend. Richard F

5/24/03 White powder gold helps with healing - check internet. The General

5/28/03 Karen Norris, Terry Metcalf

6/6/03 Brenda was here!

6/6-8/03 Worked a lot, drank a lot, slept a lot. Was pure joy! Thanks a lot, General, Paul & Chewy

5/8/03 You need to see the before pictures. Turning into a livable space. Steve Rusin

6/8/03 Remodel & renovations; ceiling, rug, shower & water tank pad, comp I tent pad, generators, lights. He's getting serious! Jim, Tino, and Paul worked their butts off -

thanks! Respect yourself, life, and this place. Thanks General. Loree Thunderbolt Wow! I fell asleep! I was here it was fun! Terra

6/8/03 Yee Haw, The General

6/8/03 Pretty neat - lots of hard work, Linda Miller & Buddy

6/11/03 - about 11 am Been here 5 days camping I working 1 drinking I 420ing and relaxing waiting for the General to return again. Enjoyed Tino's company and hard rock mining with him. Hope to work here again with Tino and stay longer here at "One Park Place" - Paradise - days have been hot but with a little breeze it's not bad at all - in the shade. Nites and mornings are perfectly cool. The cicadas or noisey bugs are very noisy in the mornings and afternoons but they are a very welcome sound. Did not see any animals, just lizards, bugs, mosquitoes and some scary humans. Keep the legend alive Flint and hopefully something very good will come of it! Thanks, Hard Rock Miner J.C.H.

6/13/03 Friday the 13th was lucky for us. Our water tank is here. Hope people appreciate and don't destroy. The General

6/13/03 Life is sure grand. I worked on stairway an around cabin. Great. Paul A. Albrecht

Wilma Huggett

Flint Carter and Wilma Huggett at the cabin in 2003.

W ilma Huggett was– if it ever existed– Western Royalty. She was born at the 3C Ranch that was, and still is, one of the largest private ranches in the Oracle area.

Wilma Huggett at the cabin in 2003.

In 1954, she was Cowgirl of the Year. Her father, Bill, took Buffalo Bill's place and took the wealthy on horseback tours to Arizona landmarks before roads were built. Bill paid $80,000 in 1928 for 160,000 acres.

Wilma was tougher than most men I ever met. She would tell you like it is in no short terms with coarse grace. There was a Huggett Room at the Oracle Historical Society, she was very wealthy and generous. Now, it is the library and a new staff member told me, no one knew who she was anyway, this is an example of newcomers rewriting history the way they see it. To leave out the Huggetts is a great insult to the pioneers who built this area! Wilma donated a wildlife corridor before she passed on. Today, it allows a safe passage for animals through Oracle.

6/16/03 Wilma Huggett, Flint Carter, David Russell and wife, and daughter. Flint and I sat here and enjoyed the peace. The Russell's went to their claim of white gold. Blessings on this place and all those who find their way here. David Russell & Tina Dear Flint, I'm very happy for the beautiful thunderbird you gave me, TAK (that means thank you in Danish) and for a great experience. Good luck to you and your nice little palace. (heart) Bine

7/18/03 Thank the Lord!!! The fire break worked! Thanks to all that helped!!! Jerry Cheatham passed on and will be missed terribly!!! He loved it here and helped very much!!! His grandfather found billions in gold in N.M. and was murdered over it, the treasure from The Mine with the Iron Door? Only Geronimo knows and he ain't tellin! The General.

The Aspen Fire 2003

The road to the cabin after the Aspen fire.

6/13/03 Things getting better here! Shower out back!
Enjoy! The General. Didn't notice smoke till late event -
watched most of the night. Left early Wednesday. Tino

The charred remains of the Aspen Fire of 2003.

The Aspen fire came within three feet to the cabin!

7/18/03 -12:20pm Fri. Wow the cabin survived, thank the Lord. The fire came within three feet of the cabin. The Aspin Fire did not consume this special place in the Santa Catalinas. Thanks again, General, for getting me here! We moved a lot of burned down trees and rocks to get here today - wow - dirty - planes overhead seeding us. We sit here having lunch and enjoying life. A lot is burned, it will return. Your friend, Jim Hicks.

Thanks for the tour John & Seth Elliott, Tucson Thanks for the mine tour. Alex & Stan Stachowiak, Tucson Thanks Keeny & Chris Mecum, Tucson Well, it's Father's Day and I'm going to see my kids. Been here since last Friday. Love it up here. Tino

8/5/03 The Van Darns rode in by horses. Took nothing - stop by to say hi.

8/13/03 Santa Catalina Trail Crew; Mike "Sunshine" Watson, Clara Peterson, Leland Vought

8/19/03 Glad it survived, Mike Watson Todd Puis, USFS - not much else did - Summerhaven is in ruins - I guess removing underbrush really helps

8/19/03 I like this place! Todd Puis. Hey General, your claim was floating away. Bottle was not weatherproof.

8/24/03 Welcome - Please enjoy internet (www.greatamericanwildwestshow.com - Cody Stone link). The General

8/24/03 I sure enjoyed it up here. Time away. A walk alone. Love it. Then they came so goodbye! Paul A. Albrecht

8/24/03 - 1:00pm Sunday. Us three stooges up here again - Nice day - Hot actually. The burned-out area is starting pretty good to return - in some areas - grass, cat claw. Buggy with flies. Had good lunch. Too hot these days up here. Won't return till winter snow we hope - lots. Maybe Thanksgiving? Still need rain! Rockhound Jim H.

9/6/03 Sat, Kurt Keller

9/6/03 Sat. Thanx, General for your hospitality!! Nathan Keller

9/06/03 With blessings for this place and the chance to be joined with the project

9/6/03 Well, General, we clear out last and the place made it, so let's hope that the hard work we did today works too. Thank you, General, for allowing me to help. Place is beautiful. Thanx. Robert J. Thompson

9/6/03 Hallelujah!! The General

10/6/03 2 more days and I'll be 56. Came here on my birthday 1978. God bless America!!!! The General

10/6/03 Bless the spirit of Buffalo Bill and Geronimo, Chocise, Kodoish, Kodoish, Kodoish, Adonai Torbayoth Joseph Michael (then ???)

10/5/03 Your comments will be in new my book "The Canyon of Gold"

10/18/03 Gold still glitters in the ground - hidden secret - like a laughing crown! Look around, there's something worth more than gold!!! God bless!!! The General

10/18/03 Love is the way I walk in Gratitude on the General's slopes of "Gold" ... and when I walk here I do not walk alone ... For he goes with me Valerie Skinner Paul Skinner

10/18/03 Once again, the wonder of this place, not just beauty, but life as beauty in all places with one heart. David Russell.

End of the Roster.

Flint Art

These pieces of art are fabricated using materials exclusively from the Santa Catalina Mountains.

Flint Carter mined, designed and fabricated Catalina Mountains art and jewelry pieces are available. Contact Flint at 520-289-4566 or Email at fintcartergold@gmail.com.

Maya.

Prickly Pear cactus.

Frog.

Mayan mask

Geronimo's Gold Table

This huge specimen found in the Catalinas weighs over 150
pounds and stands on a Saguaro base.

Turquoise thunderbird.

Our Lady of Guadalupe

Mt. Lemmon marble.

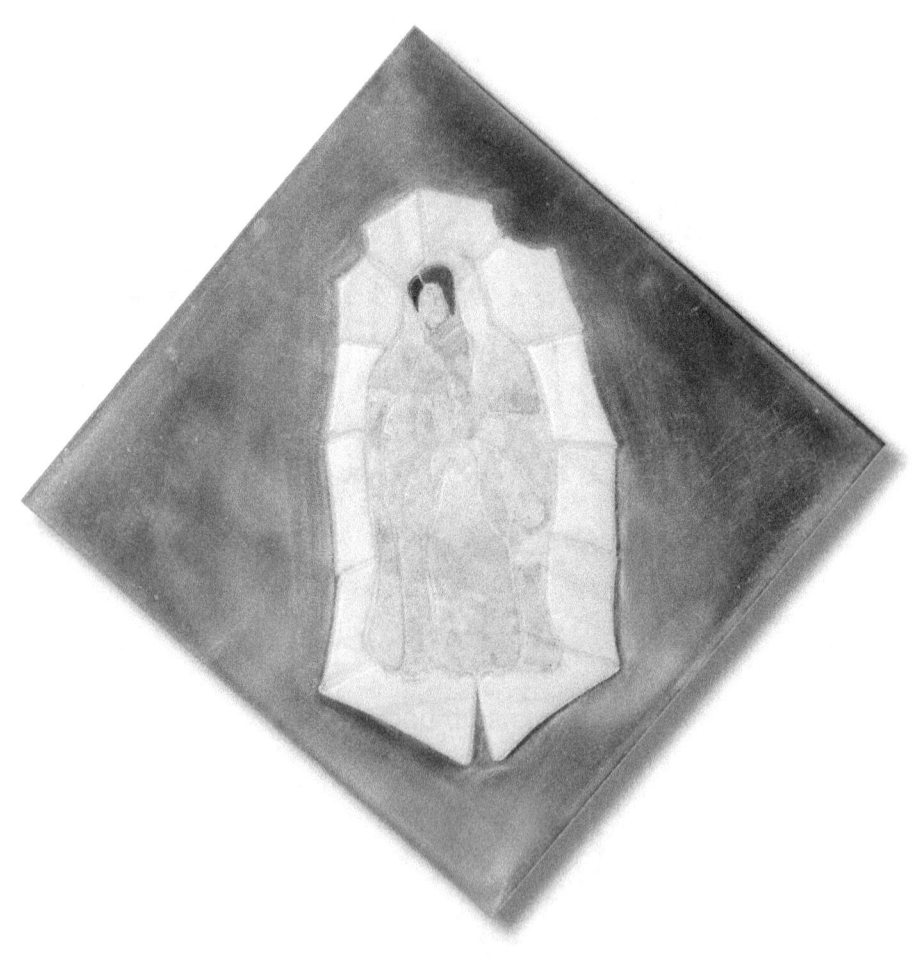

Crystal offering.

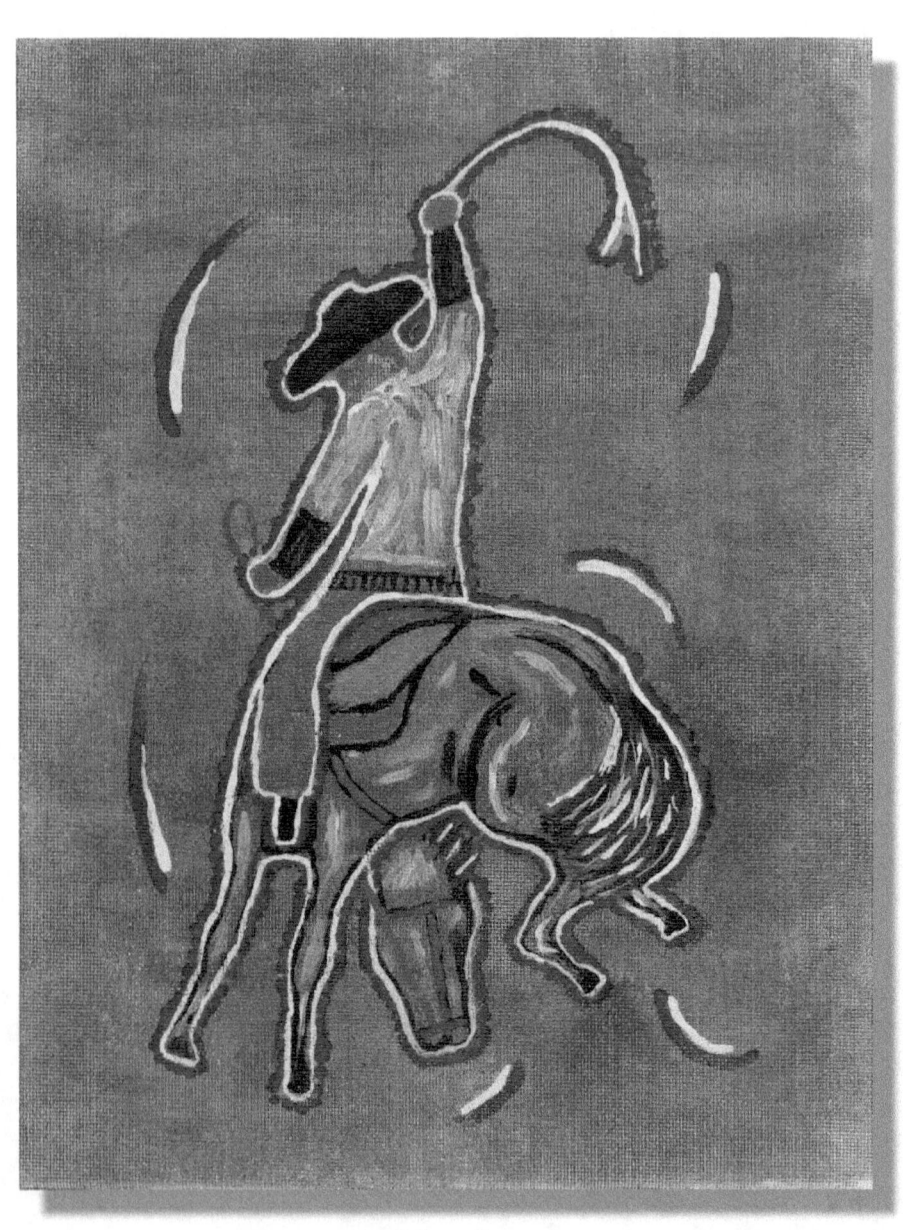

"The Cowboy," by Flint Carter

*Esmerelda: If time is silver, and blood is colored gold, Esmerelda never will grow old.

*From a song written about Tucson's legendary lost Iron Door mine.

Created by Author, Artist and Lecturer W. T. Flint Carter

Summary

This was to be the book that allowed me the chance to expose the rascals who so many times stopped my work to preserve our history. I think that will be a large book in itself and will have to wait until later.

All the thirty years plus of news articles and stories about me being a liar standing next to a hole in the ground, with this sign in roster should show the truth about my stewardship and reputation. My only worry now is that someone will destroy the cabin and all of our work.

Please enjoy the beauty and be assured there is nothing to rob. More than one person has guaranteed that the mountains' treasures will remain hidden too deep for anyone to dig up. Hopefully there will be another book to tell this epic part of history.

Thank you for your interest. Do not hesitate to contact me with questions or additions to this story.

Flint Carter: Biography

William Thomas Carter– "Flint"– to his friends, is a sophisticated primitive artist and author born in 1947 in Danville, Illinois.

After attending Danville High School, he served overseas in Panama as a military policeman during the Vietnam conflict, and received the National Defense and Good Conduct medals.

Returning home, Carter attended Danville Junior College and later Southern Illinois University. A special interest in the design department, headed by Buckminster Fuller, inspired the building of Arizona's first solar heated and cooled museum.

While in Arizona, Ted DeGrazia, whose work is now well-known in the realm of commercial art, was a mentor and a friend. He was the inspiration for the outdoor theater, "The Stage in the Sun," named in honor of DeGrazia's Gallery in the Sun.

In 1985, "The Oracle Historian" published "The Story of Gold," a short story, followed by "The Legend," a brochure produced for SaddleBrooke Development Corp, and the book, "Treasures of the Santa Catalina Mountains."

From 1995-2000, a special collection of minerals, prehistoric and historic artifacts, art, jewelry and related memorabilia from Arizona's Canyon of Gold has been shown at the Tucson Convention Center Gem and Mineral Show as an educational exhibit. For two years, the collection has premiered in the Galleria entranceway to the show.

Environmental accomplishments include a solar stucco design and a multi-million-dollar industrial toxic site clean-up.

After returning to Arizona in 1996, Carter continued to research the Iron Door Mine legend.

Flint, a seasoned prospector and miner, has held hundreds of mining claims for decades throughout the Santa Catalina Mountains, near Tucson, Arizona.

Having secured placement for various historical pieces in museums worldwide, William Thomas Carter was instrumental in returning the War Bonnet of Tasia, son of Cochise, to the Apaches at Fort Sill, Oklahoma.

Research is still being compiled. At present, an accredited archaeological discovery of a lost city involved in the Iron Door Mine legend is being documented for film and literary purposes.

Flint Carter in the Media

"Ballads of the Santa Catalina Mountains, The Mine With the Iron Door Legend," written and performed by Gary Holdcroft.

The Miners Story Project, an Oral History program of the University of Arizona has preserved Flint Carter's recollections of the Santa Catalina Mountains.

"Buffalo Bill Cody: Beyond the Legend," featuring Flint Carter telling the story of Cody's time in Arizona. Produced by Little Bighorn Productions.

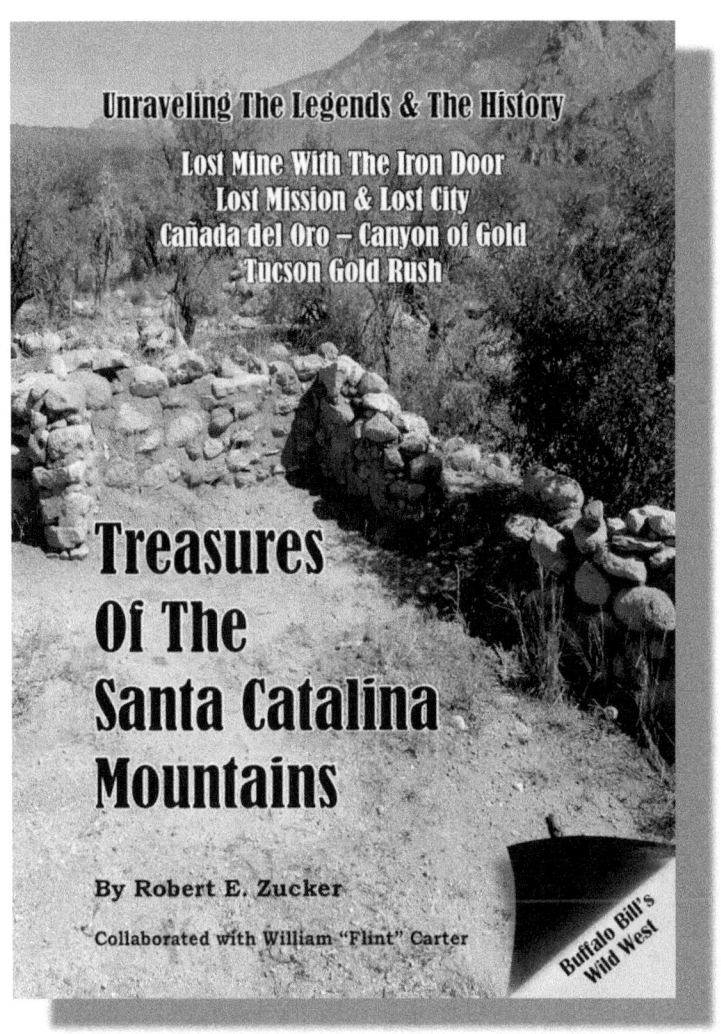

Unraveling The Legends & The History

Lost Mine With The Iron Door
Lost Mission & Lost City
Cañada del Oro – Canyon of Gold
Tucson Gold Rush

Treasures
Of The
Santa Catalina
Mountains

By Robert E. Zucker

Collaborated with William "Flint" Carter

Buffalo Bill's
Wild West

"Treasures of the Santa Catalina Mountains, Unraveling the Legends and History," by Robert E. Zucker and collaborated with Flint Carter. Available on Amazon.com, in Tucson and Oracle, Arizona businesses. Read chapters and download free PDF and purchase at emol.org/treasurescatalinas

Anyone who has information about this story or the legends of the Santa Catalina Mountains, please feel free to contact me. This is not yet over, and we learn more every day. Please help preserve our vanishing history.

To purchase more copies of this book, visit Amazon.com or contact Flint directly.

To reach Flint Carter:

Call: 520-289-4566

Email: flintcartergold@gmail.com

Web Site: http://emol.org/flintcarter/

For more books published through BZB Publishing, visit emol.org/books

www.ingramcontent.com/pod-product-compliance
Lightning Source LLC
Chambersburg PA
CBHW061502030726
47503CB00005B/1774